A NOTE FROM CADE MERRILL

In 1994 three college students went into the woods near Burkittsville, Maryland, to make a film about the legend of the Blair Witch.

They never came back.

My cousin Heather Donahue was one of those filmmakers. Heather was my favorite cousin—almost like a big sister. When she disappeared, I was only eleven years old. I couldn't accept that she was gone. Was she really dead? Was there actually a Blair Witch? I needed to find answers.

So I read every story about the Blair Witch legend that I could get my hands on. I e-mailed and called everyone who might know something about Elly Kedward, the eighteenth-century outcast some believed to be the Blair Witch, or Rustin Parr, the 1940s serial murderer who claimed that an old woman in the woods had forced him to torture and kill seven children.

It wasn't long before more people heard about my work and started sending their stories to my Web site **theblairwitchfiles.com**. Stories of strange disappearances, of family curses, of ghastly unexplained deaths. The tales are all different, but they always lead back to the Blair Witch. I researched and archived the most intriguing stories in these case files, and sealed them so that no one could exploit them for commercial or sensationalistic purposes.

The discovery of Heather's video footage in 1995 left me with more questions than answers. But it did confirm what I had come to believe—that there is something strange, something incredibly terrifying, in the Blair Woods. And its evil lives on. . . .

I am seventeen now. My case files have grown to thousands of pages. I have decided to open some of them and publish them. Why? Because I know that the answers are out there. My hope is that these books may reach that one person who holds the missing piece—the key that will unlock the mystery of the Blair Witch. If you are that person—or if you have information that may help me find the truth—please get in touch. I can be reached at **theblairwitchfiles.com**. I'm always there.

Cade Merrill
Burkittsville, MD

THE BLAIR WITCH FILES #5

THE DEATH CARD

by Cade Merrill

A Parachute Press Book

BANTAM BOOKS

NEW YORK • TORONTO • LONDON • SYDNEY • AUCKLAND

RL: 6.0, AGES 014 AND UP

THE DEATH CARD

A Bantam Book/February 2001

Books created and produced by Parachute Publishing, L.L.C.,
distributed by Random House Children's Books.
© 2001 Artisan Pictures Inc. All Rights Reserved.
Cover art copyright © 2001 by Parachute Press, Inc.

The "Stickman" is the registered trademark and service mark of
Artisan Pictures Inc. All Rights Reserved.

Look further—www.blairwitch.com

ISBN: 0-553-49366-3

Visit us on the Web! www.randomhouse.com/teens
Educators and librarians, for a variety of teaching tools, visit us at
www.randomhouse.com/teachers

Published simultaneously in the United States and Canada

Bantam Books is an imprint of Random House Children's Books, a division of
Random House, Inc. BANTAM BOOKS and the rooster colophon are registered
trademarks of Random House, Inc. Bantam Books, 1540 Broadway, New York,
New York 10036.

PRINTED IN THE UNITED STATES OF AMERICA

OPM   10   9   8   7   6   5   4   3   2   1

TO THE MEMORY
OF GAVIN BURNS.
"IT GETS US ALL
IN THE END."
R.I.P.

Acknowledgments

To JoAnn Egan Neil, without whose help and encouragement I might never have brought this case to print. Thanks also to Ferrell McDonald and Ben Rock.

THE DEATH CARD

Introduction

Last June, just before school let out for the summer, a sophomore by the name of Erin Daley approached me after one of my classes. I had been vaguely aware of her because . . . well, I thought she had a crush on me. I know that sounds conceited, but around that time Erin always seemed to show up at places where I hung out—at my locker, near my car, sometimes outside my classes. She was a nice kid and all, but not really my type. Anyway, that's not really the point. The point is, she finally stopped me after school one day to tell me what I thought was a pretty lame story about the Blair Witch.

She said her cousin, Kayla Maynard, who was a year older than she was, lived in Frederick—and she'd told Erin some ghost story that might actually be true. And afterward her cousin kept having these weird dreams.

To be honest, I wasn't really listening. There was nothing in what Erin had to say that made me think it was authentic Blair Witch material. Over the past few years I've gotten a lot of "leads" related to the Blair Witch legend and my search for answers about the disappearance of my cousin Heather Donahue. It's not unusual for someone to tell me a perfectly ordinary ghost story, tack on some detail about the Blair Witch, and then want me to investigate it. Considering that my parents still expect me to graduate from high school, I simply don't have time to check out that kind of lead. Out of necessity, I've become very selective about which stories I look into.

So when Erin came to me with Kayla's story, I assumed it was partly because Erin wanted to impress me. She told me briefly about Kayla, Kayla's mother, Sharon, and some boy named Gavin at Deep Creek Lake. It all sounded pretty questionable—especially since Deep Creek Lake is more than two hours from Burkittsville, where the whole Blair Witch legend is centered. I politely told Erin that I was really too busy to look into her story just then, and in fact, I never intended to investigate it at all.

But I know now that I made a major mistake. I wish I hadn't been so quick to dismiss Erin. I wish that when Erin first came to me, I'd taken the time to sit down with her cousin Kayla and really listen to the details of her story. And most of all, I wish I'd interviewed Sharon Maynard earlier. Maybe she wouldn't have spoken with me back then—she didn't come clean with her own daughter until it was too late. But maybe I could have convinced her.

I now realize that there were elements that seem connected to the Blair Witch legend, and it was up to me to try to piece together the truth of what really happened. I've tried to do that now, although I don't know that I've succeeded, since not all of the people involved are still alive.

I've gathered the details of this case mainly from taped interviews—237 hours' worth. I've condensed much of the material alternating Kayla's and Sharon's points of view. I've found this technique is the most effective in trying to reconstruct events in this type of case.

I should clarify for the record that Kayla prepared for her own trip to Deep Creek Lake three weeks after Erin approached me with her story. At that point, neither cousin knew any of the details of Sharon Maynard's experience back in 1974.

Like I said, when Erin first tried to talk to me that hot afternoon in June, I should have paid attention. Maybe if I had, maybe if I'd taken some kind of action, things would have turned out differently. Maybe then I wouldn't feel this terrible guilt over what happened. It's possible I might have been able to save a life. Unfortunately, I'll never know. I had no idea then that Erin Daley's crazy ghost story would eventually turn into the case file I call *The Death Card*.

PART I:

Kayla

Based on interviews with Kayla Maynard
and Erin Daley conducted
by Cade Merrill

1

Sixteen-year-old Kayla Maynard sighed in frustration as another jagged bolt of lightning sliced through the sky. "Why does it have to storm tonight?" she complained to her cousin, Erin Daley. "The biggest concert of the year—and I don't get to go, thanks to my paranoid mom." She turned away from her bedroom window in disgust.

"There'll be other concerts this summer," Erin said. She sat cross-legged on the other twin bed in Kayla's room, digging through her overnight bag for something. "What's the big deal?"

Kayla frowned at her cousin. It was funny, the two of them looked nothing alike. Kayla had short blond hair, green eyes, tanned skin, and a curvy, very feminine figure that guys tended to notice. Erin, who was a year younger, was pale and skinny with long, straight black hair, brown eyes, and silver railroad-track braces.

"The big deal is, now I won't get to see Jon," Kayla replied. Her boyfriend, Jon Prellar, had gone to the concert anyway, with one of his buddies. *Who's using my ticket,* she added to herself.

Erin grinned. "Hey, you get to have me over to spend the night. What could be more fun than that?"

"Right," Kayla said, flopping onto her bed. "At least my mom is happy. She hates Jon's hair, his earring, his tattoo, his cigarettes—everything. She just doesn't understand him, that's all. She won't even give him a chance. She refuses to trust him—or me. I was lucky she was even going to let me go to that concert tonight."

A sudden clap of thunder made Kayla and Erin both jump. "Maybe we're just meant to stay in tonight," Erin said. "It's fate."

"Yeah," Kayla agreed with a reluctant smile. "Maybe it's our karma." She didn't believe that, really. But her mom always said that everything happened for a reason and everyone was subject to an eternal justice system. Do something good—or bad—and you'd eventually get paid back for it, even if it took years. Kayla sighed again. *What had she done lately that was so bad?*

Erin finally found what she'd been scrounging for in her pack. "Look, I brought something for us to do tonight." Her dark eyes lit with excitement as she pulled out a pack of tarot cards.

"Where did you get those?" Kayla asked. "Do you know how to read them?" She'd never thought Erin was the type to get into occult stuff.

"Not very well," Erin admitted, "but I've got a book that tells you what each card means. And I know how to lay out the Celtic Cross spread."

"Okay," Kayla agreed. "There's nothing good on TV." She joined her cousin on the other bed.

Erin separated out part of the deck and shuffled it. "These are the Major Arcana, the cards that aren't part of the four suits," she explained. She fanned out the cards and held them out to Kayla. "First, you choose one to represent you. It's called the Significator."

Kayla chose a card and Erin placed it on the bedspread faceup.

"I'm an upside-down Hermit?" Kayla asked, peering at the card. "Weird."

"Hermit Reversed," Erin corrected her. She flipped through the tarot book. "Let's see. The Hermit Reversed means you're a person who's deeply involved with others."

"True," Kayla agreed, thinking of Jon.

"But it can also mean psychic disturbance," Erin

went on, frowning. "Things like bad dreams and visits from other realms."

Kayla grinned. "Okay, so I'm psychically disturbed. What else?"

"You have to shuffle the Major Arcana into the rest of the deck," Erin told her. Kayla did, then watched as Erin set the top card facedown on the Significator and arranged nine more cards in a cross-and-staff pattern surrounding the first two.

Erin picked up the card that was crossed on top of the Significator. "This covers you. That means this card is the general atmosphere that 'covers,' or surrounds, you."

"Romance if it's Jon, neurosis if it's my mother," Kayla predicted.

Erin turned up the card and gasped.

"What's the matter?" Kayla asked sharply. She stared down at a hooded skeletal figure carrying a scythe. "Death." Kayla read the name of the card aloud. "*Death* is what surrounds me?" Suddenly reading the tarot didn't seem so amusing.

"That's not necessarily what the Death Card means," Erin said quickly. "Sometimes, it has more to do with old things ending and new things beginning. Like rebirth and—here, wait a minute." She turned back to the book and thumbed through the pages again. " 'Finality, fatality, transformation, resurrection,' " she read aloud. "'A death whose effects do not end with the death but continue beyond in evil deeds.'"

Kayla shuddered. "That sounds like seriously bad karma."

Another huge thunderclap sounded directly above them. The house suddenly went dark.

"Kayla? Erin? Are you okay?" Kayla's mother called from downstairs. "I'll bring you guys some flashlights!"

"We're fine," Kayla called back to her mother, but her voice shook a little. She was still freaked out by the Death Card, even though she knew tarot cards were fake, like a Ouija board—right?

Kayla's mother hurried into the room. "Here. Turn these flashlights on!"

"Thanks, Aunt Sharon," Erin said, taking one and flipping the switch.

Kayla's mother stared down at the card on the bedspread. "What the . . . ?" she began.

"They're tarot cards," Erin answered.

Before Kayla could protest, her mother bent down and scooped up the cards. "I know what they are," she said. "And you know how I feel about anything connected to the occult."

"Mom!" Kayla cried. "Give us a break. They're just for fun."

"Erin, I'll give the cards back to you before you go home," Kayla's mother said. "I'm sorry, but I won't have you reading them in this house. Maybe you two should come downstairs with me. I've got hurricane lamps lit in the living room. We could all play a nice game of Monopoly or—"

Kayla rolled her eyes. "We're fine, Mom. Really. We're not little kids."

"But you don't understand," her mother began. "I know things you—" She stopped suddenly and bit her lip. Then she looked down at the cards in her hands. "Sorry, girls," she said finally, handing them back to Erin. "I don't know what came over me. I guess I overreacted. Don't stay up too late, okay?" She left, leaving Kayla's bedroom door slightly open. That was a rule in the Maynard house. *No secrets*, her mother always insisted.

"Whoa," Kayla said, shaking her head. She didn't feel so creeped out by the tarot cards now. She was more freaked by her mom's weird behavior. "I don't know why she acted that way," Kayla told her cousin. "Sorry."

Erin shrugged. "No problem. Tarot cards are pretty dumb, anyway." She tucked the tarot cards back into her overnight bag. Secretly Kayla felt relieved. In *her* opinion they were totally creepy.

"You know, you and your mom are a lot alike sometimes," Erin said.

"What do you mean?" Kayla asked.

Erin hesitated. "Well, you both get pretty emotional about stuff. And you look so much like she did when she was your age. I mean, the first time I saw that high school yearbook photo of her, I thought it was you with a really bad haircut. Maybe she looks at you and gets terrified you'll make all the same mistakes she did."

"Ha! My mom never made mistakes. You know that," Kayla said. "So anyway, what are we going to do now?"

Erin shrugged. "How about ghost stories?" She leaned forward. "Here, I'll start. . . . There's this girl who goes on a blind date with this guy. He walks her to the door at the end of the night. The girl thinks he's going to kiss her. He reaches out to touch her cheek, only he doesn't have a hand. It's a hook. He digs it into her neck and blood starts spurting out everywhere and the girl dies."

"That's it?" Kayla asked. "That's the end?"

Erin nodded.

"Pretty lame," Kayla said.

"Come up with something better, then," Erin challenged.

"Okay." Kayla thought fast. She reached for the first image that came to mind.

"There were a bunch of kids at summer camp," she began. "Out in the woods. They were hiking near a place called Deep Creek Lake. As they walked, the leaves and twigs they stepped on made horrible

13

crunching noises, like they were stepping on the skeletons of the countless dead buried beneath them. . . ."

"Cool," Erin said.

Kayla paused. The words were coming from her mouth, but she had no idea what would come out next. It was almost as if someone else were telling the story *through* her.

"The kids began to hear other sounds," Kayla went on. "Strange sounds they didn't recognize. The kids wondered if all the terrible stories they'd heard were true."

"What stories?" Erin wanted to know.

Kayla frowned. Actually, she hadn't a clue. But then she went on, almost without thinking. "They'd heard that the Blair Witch—and her terrible evil— had spread from the Black Hills Forest, all the way to Deep Creek Lake."

"The Blair Witch?" Erin interrupted. "How does *she* get into the story?"

Kayla paused. She didn't know much about the Blair Witch, except for a movie she'd rented once. Her mom had made her return it to the video store, right in the middle. "It's just the way the story goes," she told her cousin helplessly. "So anyway, two of the campers slipped away from the group, a boy and a girl. No one else noticed that they were gone. They waited until the others were far ahead of them, and then they went in search of the witch—"

"Kayla, this isn't funny." Erin's voice was sharp. "I *live* in Burkittsville, remember? The Blair Witch isn't a joke."

"I know," Kayla said. "I'm not trying to be funny."

"Then why are you telling this whole stupid thing?"

"Because I have to," Kayla answered, realizing that she was telling the truth. She didn't know where the story was coming from. She just knew she had to tell it.

"The boy told the girl that their lives were in danger. But they headed toward the bog anyway. It was a dry, sunny day. The bog was shrouded in fog, and the air that surrounded it seemed dark and ominous. Mysterious sounds filled the air, like children screaming—"

"I don't want to hear this," Erin protested, covering her ears. "Shut up!"

Kayla was feeling a little spooked herself, but she couldn't stop. She had to go on with the story. "Because of the darkness, neither one saw the fallen logs that lay in front of them. They fell, tumbling over each other, scattering the precious contents of their backpacks across the muddy ground. Frantically they tried to retrieve their things. Otherwise, they would definitely be killed. That's when they heard a high-pitched scream behind them. The girl stood frozen with fear. It sounded like someone being strangled.

15

The boy grabbed his pack and started running, knowing it was the witch. And then he realized he couldn't move. His feet had become stuck in the bog. He cried to the girl for help. But the girl just stood and stared—"

Erin was wincing. "I swear, Kayla, I'm never sleeping over here again."

Kayla jumped off the bed and ran to the window. She looked out into the stormy darkness. ". . . And then the girl watched as a strange, heavy fog appeared. Slowly the fog took the shape of a cloaked woman. An old hag. The hag swept over to the boy. The boy tried to plead with the woman, but it was useless. The awful hag wrenched the boy's head from his writhing body."

"Oh, gross! Kayla, stop!" Erin cried.

"I can't," Kayla told her, trembling now. "The story isn't done. Because then the witch turned to the girl, and she—"

"No!" a strangled voice called from the doorway. "Not another word!"

2

Kayla and Erin whirled around. Kayla's mother was standing at the door, her horrified face bathed in an eerie light from the flashlight in her hand.

"Mom!" Kayla cried. "You scared us!"

"Where did you hear that story?" her mother demanded, coming into the room. She shook Kayla's shoulders. "Tell me. Where did you hear it?"

Kayla was used to her mother being a worrier, but this went way beyond her usual paranoia. "Mom, were you eavesdropping on us?"

Her mother looked defensive. "Of course not. I was passing by in the hall. Anyway, that's not what matters. I want to know where you heard that story."

"I just made it up," Kayla answered, still trying to

figure out why her mother was acting so weird. She'd never seen her like this.

"Don't give me that. Where did you hear it?"

"I swear, I just made it up," Kayla insisted. "You heard me, Erin, right?"

Erin nodded, looking unhappy. She clearly didn't want to be in the middle of this.

"Why does that story freak you out so much?" Kayla pressed. She didn't add, It freaked me out, too. "You're acting as if the whole thing were true or something."

"It is," her mother said. Then she said slowly, "I mean, it's not actually *true*, but . . ."

"But what?" Kayla practically shouted.

"It's j-just, well . . . ," her mother stammered. "It's just that it's vaguely similar to something that happened to some kids I knew when I was in high school."

"Similar? A witch pulling a guy's head off?"

Her mother waved a hand. "Oh, you know what I mean," she said. She gave Kayla and Erin a weak grin.

This isn't making any sense, Kayla thought. Her mother was always so . . . *logical*. "C'mon, Mom, tell us," she urged. "Who were the kids that this happened to?"

"This is getting ridiculous," her mother said, but her voice sounded brittle. Kayla realized her mother was trembling. "Why don't you girls go to bed now?"

"Okay." Erin spoke up quickly. "Night, Aunt Sharon." Kayla had a feeling her cousin had had enough of the whole witch thing.

"Good night," Kayla echoed. Obviously, her mother wasn't going to tell them anything. "That was so bizarre," she whispered to Erin after her mom had left. "It's like she's hiding some big secret."

Erin began changing into a pair of pajamas with little Day-Glo hearts on them. "So Kayla, where *did* that story come from?" she asked. "Tell me the truth."

Kayla went over and closed the window. The wind had suddenly picked up, blowing the filmy white curtains. "I swear, I don't know. Suddenly it was just in my mind. And the weird thing is that as I was telling it, I could see every scene so clearly. Like I was watching it in a movie." She shivered, trying to erase the images from her mind.

Erin was silent for a moment. "There is a real Deep Creek Lake, isn't there?" she said finally.

"Yeah," Kayla replied. "Jon asked me to go snowboarding with him there in February. And my mom said 'No way.' As in, 'No way in this lifetime or any other.' "

"That's because your mother hates Jon," Erin pointed out.

"Maybe," Kayla said slowly. "Or maybe it's because she didn't want me going to Deep Creek Lake.

If what she told us was true, something bad must have happened there when she was my age. Something that scared her so much she won't even tell me what it is."

"That's really creepy," Erin said, crawling under the covers. "Let's not talk about it anymore, okay?"

But Kayla wasn't listening. "Somehow, I've got to get my mother to tell me what happened," she said.

"Mmm," Erin said. She sounded half-asleep already.

In the dim glow of her flashlight, Kayla started getting ready for bed. She suddenly remembered something and padded over to her closet.

"Where is that T-shirt Jon brought back for me?" she muttered to herself. It said EXTREME SNOWBOARD-ING AT WISP. DEEP CREEK LAKE, MARYLAND. Maybe if she wore it in the morning, it would jog her mom's memory.

Kayla dug through the folded stack of T-shirts on the top shelf, then rummaged through the clothes on the second shelf. "Where is it?" she asked herself. "I *know* it was in the dirty clothes Mom just washed. She should have put it in here this morning when she brought the laundry up." Kayla would just have to go downstairs and check the dryer.

Taking the flashlight, she crept down to the first floor and crossed the dark house to the utility room. She searched through the hamper filled with dirty clothes, then through the clean clothes stacked neatly on top of the dryer. Nothing.

Ready to give up, Kayla aimed her flashlight at the wastebasket tucked beneath the shelves that held the detergent and softener. There she spotted the Deep Creek Lake T-shirt. Only she wouldn't be able to wear it tonight—or ever.

It was ripped to shreds.

Torn and cut into a dozen ragged pieces, all of them stained bloodred.

NOTE FROM CADE MERRILL: *While it's theoretically possible that Kayla made up the story she told her cousin that night, it's interesting to note that she used the phrase ". . . the awful hag wrenched the boy's head from his writhing body. . . ." This is taken verbatim from* The Blair Witch Cult, *a book published in 1809, the only known copy of which is located in the Maryland Historical Society in Baltimore. Most of the book is pretty unreadable because the paper has rotted away. In any case, it's hard to imagine that Kayla, who claims she had no prior interest in the Blair Witch, would know the book existed, much less be quoting from it.*

3

The boy was tall and lanky, with a thin, pinched, pale face and long, shaggy blond hair. He wore tight, faded jeans and a black T-shirt that said PLAGUE *across the front. He was holding a tarot card—the Death Card—in front of him. It showed a scythe-wielding skeleton.*

"Well, hello again," the boy said, smiling. "Remember me?"

Kayla woke with a start, shaking. She could only recall a fragment of her dream, but it was enough. The boy with the Death Card. The exact same boy she'd pictured in her mind when she'd told her ghost story to Erin the night before. And the Death Card—well, that part of the dream must have come from messing with Erin's tarot deck. In the dream, the Death Card was even scarier than the one in Erin's deck.

Kayla sat up in bed and glanced across the room. Erin was still sound asleep. Good, she thought. She needed to have a talk with her mother.

She found her sitting at the kitchen table, finishing her morning coffee. Her mom looked as if she hadn't slept all night. Her face was tight and drawn. There were deep, dark circles beneath her eyes, and her usually perfect blond hair looked greasy.

"Guess the electricity's back," Kayla said, nodding at the automatic-drip coffeemaker.

Her mother looked a bit startled. "What? Oh, yes, coffee. Thank goodness. I'd be a wreck without my morning java."

"Mom, I need to ask you something," Kayla said. She held up the shredded Deep Creek Lake T-shirt. "Did you do this?"

"Oh, that. Well, I . . . I, um, put it in with the colors by mistake. I'd left a lipstick in the pocket of my jeans, and it ruined everything," she explained. "I forgot to tell you. I'm really sorry, honey. I just threw it out."

"After you ripped it into shreds?"

Her mother just stared at her, her expression unreadable.

"Mom, why would you do something like this? Is

it because Jon gave it to me?" She paused. "Or because it says 'Deep Creek Lake'?"

Her mother immediately got up from the table and put her coffee mug in the dishwasher. "I've got a few errands to run, honey, but I made a fruit salad for you and Erin. It's in the fridge. And there's bacon and eggs and cereal—"

"Deep Creek Lake freaks you out for some reason, doesn't it?"

"Kayla, I told you. The T-shirt got ruined in the wash. End of story. If I'm not back by the time your aunt comes for Erin, tell her I'll call her tonight."

But Kayla wouldn't be put off. "What *really* happened to those kids you knew?" she demanded.

"Nothing." Her mother's voice was barely audible. Kayla noticed that she was gripping the back of a chair so tightly that her knuckles had gone white.

Kayla was sure her mother was lying. But why? "Come on, Mom," she pleaded. "You're always saying we should never keep secrets from each other. Just tell me."

Her mother shut her eyes for a moment. When she opened them, she took a deep breath. "All right," she said finally. "A friend of mine, a girl I went to high school with, spent a week in 4-H camp at Deep Creek Lake one summer. There was a boy there who was—oh, I don't know—different. Gavin something, I think his name was. Some of the kids made fun of him because he kept talking about the Blair Witch. And then . . . there was an accident."

"You mean, the witch got the boy?" Kayla asked.

"No. Of course not," her mother answered. "Don't be silly. Give it a rest, Kayla. This all happened a long time ago."

"So what kind of accident?" Kayla pressed. Her mother was definitely hiding something. She was sure of it.

"Look, that's all I know," her mother told her. "Okay? Now I've got to go. I have a million errands to run. We'll talk later." She kissed Kayla on the forehead, then left before her daughter could ask any more questions.

PART II:

Sharon—Summer 1974

*Based on taped interviews with Sharon Maynard
(née Webster) and from research of Frederick,
Maryland, 4-H camp records dated
July 23–27, 1974*

4

I had just turned sixteen the summer my parents decided to send me to the 4-H Center at Deep Creek Lake in western Maryland. At first I didn't want to go. I thought the four H's—Head, Heart, Hands, and Health—sounded pretty corny. It wasn't that I was from a big city or anything. Frederick's population was only about thirty thousand back then. I just wasn't a farm kid, which is how I thought of 4-H Clubs. But by the time school finished for the year and the first few weeks of June went by, I realized I couldn't wait to go to 4-H, or anywhere, really. A week without parents suddenly seemed like a great idea.

MY THIRD NIGHT at camp I suddenly awoke to the sound of terrified screams.

I heard a thump as Alison, the girl who slept in the bunk on top of mine, jumped down to the floor. "Somebody, please help me!" Alison screamed.

Marie Walters, our counselor, flipped on the lights in the cabin. "What's going on?" she asked.

"Get off me!" Alison screamed again. She was shaking violently, slapping at her arms and legs, pulling at her hair and face.

And then the rest of us started screaming, too.

Thick, slimy black bugs slithered up and down Alison's body. They were all over her face, trying to crawl into her eyes and mouth.

"They're biting me!" Alison screamed.

"Calm down, all of you!" Marie shouted. She pulled on her hiking boots and grabbed a pillowcase.

With her hand inside the pillowcase for protection, Marie began pulling the bugs off Alison, stomping them as they hit the floor. But the bugs left a horrible black slime on Alison's body, and a rancid stench filled the cabin.

"Carolyn, get me a cool, damp washcloth," Marie ordered.

Alison was trembling violently, tears running

down her face. "They kept biting me," she sobbed. "Are th-they—poisonous?"

"Of course not!" Marie frowned as she took the washcloth from Carolyn. Gently she began to wash the black slime off Alison's skin. "I've never seen anything like this," she admitted. "They look like box elder bugs, but box elders don't attack people. And this gross slime . . ." She shook her head.

By then all of us were out of our bunks, hysterically examining ourselves for bugs.

My friend Kathy stared at the slime-streaked floor. "I can't sleep in here tonight with these massacred bugs," she announced. "They're too gross."

I shuddered. "Yeah. How do we know Marie killed them all? What if there are more—hiding in our sheets or under the floorboards?"

"Can we go home?" Carolyn asked. "My dad will come pick us up."

"Okay, everyone, let's not panic," Marie said. "This is what we'll do. You're all going to get dressed. Then we'll head up to the main lodge. We'll figure out the next step once we're there. Bring your flashlights and your toothbrushes." She turned to Alison. "Come on, Allie," she said gently. "Let's get some clothes on you."

Marie practically had to carry a sobbing Alison to the lodge. The rest of us trailed behind, silent and

31

scared. Carolyn had the right idea, I thought. We should all go home. The truth was, this place had been creeping me out since I'd arrived. I didn't know why, exactly. It was just a feeling.

Marie consulted with some of the other counselors about what to do. It was past midnight and everyone was tired. Allie said she was too frightened to sleep. Marie agreed to take her to the infirmary and stay with her through the night.

"What about the rest of us?" Carrie asked indignantly. "We're not going back to that cabin, either."

"Tell you what," said a counselor named Mike. "You girls come with me. We'll put you in another cabin for tonight."

He led the four of us to Cabin G.

"Isn't this one of the boys' cabins?" I asked.

"That's right," Mike said. "But four of the eight beds are empty in there. We always have more girls than boys at camp," he explained. "Don't worry, it will just be for tonight."

The lights inside the cabin were on when we arrived, and the four boys were wide awake. My heart sank when I realized that one of them was Gavin Burns.

Gavin and I had sat on the bus together from Frederick County to the 4-H Center. I figured out pretty fast that Gavin was . . . well . . . weird. Tall and scrawny, with long, shaggy blond hair, Gavin looked like a roadie for a heavy-metal band. He wore tight, ripped jeans and a faded Plague concert T-shirt. Plague was a rock band with a reputation for being connected to the occult. There were all sorts of creepy rumors that the reason they topped the charts was because one of them had made a deal with the devil.

Gavin had three major strikes against him. He had an odd, formal way of speaking; he believed in weird stuff, like every dark rumor about Plague; and he had absolutely no sense of humor. He took everything super-seriously. Needless to say, I was not thrilled when he sat next to me on the bus and started trying to impress me. I wished he would just disappear. Otherwise, I might end up being a social reject like him—before we even reached camp.

Now, as I walked over to a bed on the far side of the cabin and put down my things, I could feel Gavin staring at me. His beady eyes were practically boring straight through me. Great, I thought. I get to spend a whole night with Weirdo.

I breathed a sigh of relief when Mike tied a rope across the middle of the cabin and hung sheets across it, forming a curtain to separate the girls' side from the boys'.

"Listen up, everyone," Mike called from the boys' side of the cabin. "I've got to go take care of that bug problem in the girls' bunk. Steve from Cabin B will be here in a few minutes. So do me a favor and just go to sleep, okay?"

Everyone agreed. But moments after Mike left, Carl Wagner poked his head around our side of the curtain. "Welcome to Cabin G," he said, smiling at us. "How about we all play a game of cards? Like strip poker!"

"Dream on, loser," Kathy told him.

"Let's tell ghost stories," Carolyn suggested.

The boys seemed to think that was an okay idea, although Gavin didn't really say anything. He just stared at me like a lovesick puppy when we girls went over to the other side of the curtain. I totally ignored him.

We all sat in a circle. Carrie went first. Her story was about a boy trapped in a haunted attic. Then Carl and another boy named Stu took their turns, telling stories with lots of blood, guts, and brains being splattered across walls. Finally it was my turn.

I wasn't sure what to say. Everyone was staring at me expectantly.

I took a deep breath. "This is a true story," I began. "About Frederick County's very own Blair Witch." I told them the strange things that had happened in an area near my hometown in 1786.

"The children disappeared one by one. No trace of them was ever found. A woman named Elly Kedward had been banished from Blair more than a year earlier and left for dead in the middle of the winter. But the townspeople still believed she was a witch and that she was to blame. They claimed that she'd somehow survived to get her revenge. The Blair Witch had many victims, but she seemed to prefer the young and those she believed had wronged her. Especially those brave enough to question her evil . . ."

The cabin was quiet when I finished. I could tell that my story had impressed everyone. Except Gavin. He had a strange expression on his face that I couldn't quite read.

As Carolyn started to tell her story, Gavin came to sit beside me. "That was quite a story," he whispered. "I take it you don't believe in the Blair Witch."

I rolled my eyes. "No one does. It's just a legend."

"It's not," Gavin insisted. "You have to believe in her, Sharon. Because she's here at Deep Creek Lake. We all need to be extremely careful." He lowered his voice. "And the worst thing is not to believe in the witch. That makes her *really* mad."

I sighed. "It's a stupid *ghost* story, Gavin. You don't have to take everything so seriously."

"This *is* serious," Gavin insisted, leaning so close that he was practically spitting in my face.

"Don't worry, Gavin," I told him, inching away. "We're two hours from Burkittsville. The witch doesn't do 4-H camps."

"Fine. Don't believe me," Gavin said. He went back to his place on the other side of the circle to sulk. He refused to tell a story, but no one cared.

Gavin Burns was just a nerd.

>✠<

THE NEXT MORNING Marie and Mike took a group of us out to see Swallow Falls. It was an unusually hot day. I was dragging behind, feeling tired after not getting much sleep the night before. Gavin kept looking back at me. *What is his problem?* I wondered. I wished he'd pick some other girl to drool over. Why me?

I tried to pick up my pace, but my legs ached and I had no energy. The group was getting farther and farther ahead of me.

I forced myself to walk faster. But I started having trouble breathing. I tried to catch my breath but couldn't. Soon I was gasping. I couldn't seem to get any air into my lungs.

Then I felt something tighten around my neck, cutting into my windpipe. *What's happening?* I wondered frantically. I reached for my throat, but there was nothing there.

The trees seemed to circle around and around me. *I'm being strangled,* I thought. Then everything became a blur, and I passed out.

5

"I warned you, Sharon. I *warned* you."

Those were the first words I heard when I opened my eyes.

Gavin was standing directly over me. "I told you the witch was here," he said.

Mike pushed Gavin out of the way and kneeled down beside me. "Are you okay?" he asked.

I gingerly felt my throat. The terrifying pressure was gone. I could actually breathe normally now. "I think so," I answered.

Mike helped me to my feet. "Well, let's get you to the infirmary and make sure," he said.

Twenty minutes later I was sitting on an examining table while Loretta McCormick, the nurse on duty, put a wet towel across my forehead and took my blood pressure and pulse. Then she peered into my eyes and ears and down my throat.

"I didn't see any history of asthma on your health form. I'd say you passed out from the heat," the nurse said. "Although I'm not sure what these are." She handed me a mirror and pointed to my neck.

I gulped. Sure enough, there were faint—but very definite—red lines across my throat, as if someone *had* tried to strangle me. Was Gavin right after all about the witch? But why would she come after *me*?

Don't be stupid, I told myself, handing the nurse back the mirror. But I couldn't shake the feeling that something was terribly wrong. Evil.

"I'll have to call your parents," the nurse said.

"No, please don't!" I protested. "If my mom finds out I fainted, she'll take me home. And she'll watch over me like a hawk for the rest of the summer." That would be worse than 4-H camp, no matter how creepy the place was.

"I'm sorry, Sharon," the nurse said. "But for serious matters—and passing out is considered quite serious—camp regulations require me to notify your parents."

"But *you* said it wasn't serious," I argued. "You said I just got a little overheated."

She looked at me doubtfully.

"Please," I said. "Can't you just tell them I got a little sick? Like, from bad camp food?"

"No, I won't lie to your parents," the nurse said. "But I will tell them that, in my opinion, it was just a little heat spell, and I expect you'll be fine. On one condition."

"What's that?" I asked.

"That you sleep for a while this afternoon."

I promised that I would. I was happy to, actually. I took a nice long nap in the infirmary's outer office, where the air conditioner blew cool air across my face. But as I fell asleep, Gavin's voice played through my mind: *I warned you, Sharon. I warned you.*

THAT EVENING IN the dining hall I joined Kathy, Carrie, and Carolyn at our usual table.

"Allie went home today," Carolyn told me. "She didn't want to finish out the week. So what happened to you during the hike?"

I just shrugged. I didn't feel like getting into the whole thing. "It was the heat, I guess. The nurse said I didn't have enough fluids. I blacked out."

"Is that all?" Carrie asked. She sounded disappointed.

"Well . . ." I hesitated. It was kind of cool being the center of attention. "Gavin Burns didn't think it was the heat. He said it was the Blair Witch. He said she's come to kill us all!" I wiggled my fingers, pretending to be a scary ghost. "Woooooo!"

"Gavin's nuts," Carrie said. "He's obviously listened to one too many Plague albums."

"I say we teach him a lesson," Carolyn said. "Why don't we play a joke on Gavin to make him believe the witch has come to get him?"

"Count me in," Kathy said.

I hesitated for a minute, remembering the red marks on my neck. I didn't want anything to do with Gavin or his stupid witch.

"Come on, Sharon," Kathy said, nudging me. "Maybe you can scare that Witch Boy away. He'll never bother you again."

Well, *that* sounded good. "Okay," I said, nodding. "I'm in, too."

Just as the words left my mouth, Gavin came up to our table.

"Sharon, are you okay?" he asked. I felt my face go red with embarrassment.

"Can I see those red marks on your neck?" he asked, coming closer. He leaned down to touch my throat.

I pushed him away. "Don't touch me!"

"Ooooh," Carrie said. "Marks on her neck? Now they're getting romantic."

"Shut up!" I sputtered.

"I'm just concerned, that's all," Gavin said. He turned to the other girls. "I don't know if Sharon told you, but I think she needs to be extra careful. We all do. There's evil here."

I watched, mortified, as the other girls tried to keep straight faces. I actually felt sorry for Gavin. Almost. He sounded proud to be sharing this information, as if he were my big protector. But he was so pathetic.

He turned back and looked me squarely in the eye. "Please don't do anything stupid, Sharon," he said. "Enjoy your dinner." Then he tipped an imaginary hat and walked away.

"Oh, my God, what a *freak*!" Kathy said.

"And he's in *loooove* with Sharon," Carrie teased.

I felt my face turning bright red again. Gavin was beyond an annoying pest now. He was humiliating me. I looked down at the fried chicken on my plate—and suddenly had a brilliant idea.

"Okay, guys, listen up," I said. "It's time to start planning that joke."

><

AFTER LIGHTS-OUT we sneaked away from our fumigated cabin. I was the last one out, moving more slowly than the others, because I was draped head to toe in blankets.

Kathy dropped back to walk beside me. "You okay?"

"I feel like a little kid dressed up for Halloween."

"Well, you look creepy in the moonlight," Kathy assured me.

"Good," I said.

We reached the boys' cabins and circled round to the back of Cabin G. Carrie pointed to the window on the left. "That's the one above Gavin's bed," she whispered.

Kathy and Carolyn knelt down in the dirt so that I could step on their backs and reach the window. Fortunately, because of the heat, the window was already open. I pushed it ever so slightly and poked my head in. I could just see the faint outline of Gavin's scrawny body beneath his blanket. I reached my hand down to Carrie.

"Drop them one at a time," Carrie said as she handed me the chicken bones we had saved from dinner. "Try and get them right in front of his face," she whispered.

I dropped the first bone. It landed on Gavin's pillow, but he didn't budge. I dropped another one. It barely missed hitting his nose. Still, he didn't stir.

I turned back to my friends. "This isn't working," I called. "It's time for desperate measures. Can you boost me higher?"

"What are you going to do?" Carrie asked.

"I'm going in," I replied grimly.

I lifted one leg onto the sill, and then the other,

carefully maneuvering myself to the side of Gavin's bed. He was sleeping with his back turned to me.

I leaned over, and in the scariest voice I could muster, I whispered in his ear, "This is the Blair Witch, Gavin. You were right. I *am* here at 4-H camp. And I've come to kill *you*!" I grabbed his shoulder and pulled him toward me. Gavin's face was revealed in the moonlight. To my horror, I realized that it was too late.

Gavin's frozen eyes burned into mine. He was already dead!

PART III:

The Deep Creek Lake Project

Based on taped interviews with Kayla Maynard, Erin Daley, and Jon Prellar and on video footage

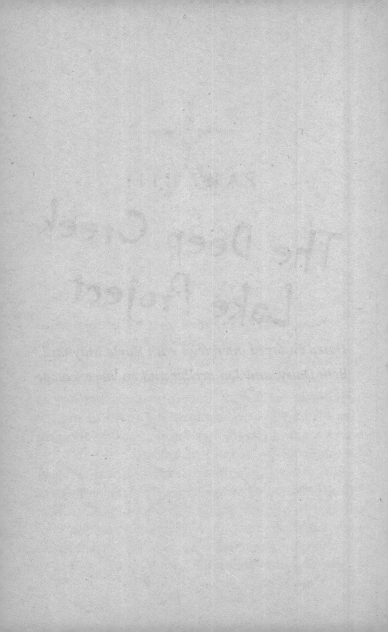

6

Kayla set her overstuffed tote in the open trunk of Jon's hand-me-down Volvo and tried to calm the butterflies in her stomach. She'd been sick with dread from the moment she woke up. This was it. Today was the day. Her mom was visiting Kayla's grandpa for the weekend. And she and Erin and Jon were standing outside her house, packing Jon's car for their trip—to Deep Creek Lake.

Erin walked up to Kayla, video camera in hand. "This is Erin Daley for the Deep Creek Lake Project," she said in her best Diane Sawyer style. "I am here with Kayla Maynard, project director, and Jon Prellar, transport specialist, and we are preparing for a journey into the wilds of western Maryland.

Ms. Maynard, could you explain the goal of this expedition?"

Kayla winced. "Cut it out, Erin. It's not funny."

"Seriously then," Erin said, dropping the fake voice. "This whole trip was your idea. If we're going to record it, you should tell us why you're so set on going."

"Okay." Kayla stared into the camera. "I want to go to Deep Creek Lake and find out why my mom gets so weird whenever I mention the place."

But that wasn't the only reason, Kayla thought. It was also because of the *dreams*.

Ever since the night when she'd told Erin that ghost story, she'd been having weird dreams. And they seemed so . . . *real*.

There was always a strange boy in them. He told her his name was Gavin. He was tall and thin, with shaggy blond hair, and wore tight, faded jeans and a Plague T-shirt. She wasn't sure, but she thought they were a real-life heavy metal band—a long time ago.

The scary part was, sometimes the boy was holding a tarot card. The Death Card. But it was different than the one in Erin's deck. He kept talking about a bog. And begging for help. She could *feel* him calling to her, like a cold ocean current, pulling her out to sea.

Even in broad daylight Kayla couldn't help shuddering. Last night the boy had said, "You'll find the witch at Deep Creek Lake. You know that, don't you? You've known all along."

"Mr. Prellar?" Erin said, breaking into Kayla's thoughts. She turned the camera on Jon.

"I don't do interviews," he told her, putting his hand over the lens. "Besides"—he slid Kayla a sideways look—"my reasons for going are strictly personal."

Kayla felt herself blushing. Jon was leaning against the side of the Volvo, his arms now folded across his chest. Even when he was just standing there, Kayla found him incredibly hot. He had thick, glossy dark hair, light gray eyes, and a lean, hard body. She could live with the fact that he wasn't really interested in Deep Creek Lake. What mattered was that Jon Prellar wanted to spend the weekend with her.

Erin offered Kayla the camera. "You want to film me?"

"Sure," Kayla said, focusing the lens on her cousin. "How do you feel about this trip?"

"Kinda nervous," Erin admitted.

Jon groaned. "Don't tell me you believe that witch stuff, too?"

"I'm open to the possibility," Erin admitted. "In Burkittsville you hear a lot of stories about the Blair Witch. A lot of people believe in her."

"Yeah, and a lot of people believe in UFOs and little green men," Jon replied.

"Cynic," Kayla said, and turned off the camera.

"Big time," Jon assured her. He hooked an arm around her shoulders and drew her close. "Look, I'm okay with driving us up there, but don't expect me to believe this witch crap. The only reason I'm going is because I want to be with you."

Erin tucked her sleeping bag into the trunk. "Maybe it's good you don't believe," she said. "We need at least one person who isn't spooked from the start."

Kayla just stared up at Jon. He always seemed so sure of himself. Nothing scared him. He assumed he'd always land on his feet, and he was usually right. Up until today she'd found that sexy, reassuring. Now she couldn't help wondering if he was wrong. Maybe he ought to be scared. What if she was drawing both Jon and Erin into something that none of them would be able to handle?

"What?" Jon asked her with a grin. "What's with all these worried looks?" He bent his head and kissed her.

"A-hem." Erin cleared her throat loudly. "Sorry to interrupt, but, Kayla, how are we going to carry all of our supplies if all you have is that?" She pointed at Kayla's trendy little Kate Spade tote. Kayla's shorts, underwear, and hairbrush were already spilling out of it. "Do you know *anything* about the outdoors?"

"Not much," Kayla admitted. "I'm not exactly the

granola type. But I did get these cool new boots." She held up one foot, proudly displaying a new Timberland. "Besides, I studied some maps of the area. Back in 1974 you had to hike to get to anything. Now there are all these fire roads. One of them takes us right up near the bog—that's the place the boy in my dreams keeps talking about. It'll be a short hike from where we park the car."

Jon snorted. "Boy in your dreams," he mimicked. "That should be *me*, babe."

Kayla ignored him.

"Do you at least have a duffel bag you could carry your stuff in?" Erin asked her.

"Wait, yeah. I think I saw a real backpack in the basement when I was getting the sleeping bags. I'll be right back." Kayla grabbed her tote and hurried into the house.

She opened the door to the basement and reached up for the string that turned on the light. Kayla muttered a curse as it came off in her hand. She grabbed one of her mom's many flashlights from a kitchen drawer, then started for the basement a second time. Clearly, it was going to be one of those days.

Kayla had never liked going into the basement. It was chilly and damp and everything in it smelled of mildew. I'll just get the pack and get out of here, she told herself.

She walked over to where she remembered seeing

the backpack wedged behind a stack of boxes. The boxes were covered with a thick layer of dust. Like most of what was in the basement, they looked as if they hadn't been opened in a hundred years. Why didn't her mother just toss this stuff?

Kayla pulled a few of the boxes out of the way and reached over to grab one of the backpack's padded straps. She lifted it up and over and set it down in front of her. The pack wasn't heavy, but it was big and bulky with a metal frame. She batted off the dust that had gathered on top and slung it over her shoulder.

She was halfway up the stairs when she heard the sound of a door slamming shut. She looked up.

"What the—?" Kayla muttered. She ran to the top of the stairs and turned the knob, but the basement door didn't budge. It was stuck.

"Jon? Erin? Can you hear me?" she called, but no one answered. Weird, she thought.

There's got to be a way out, Kayla told herself. She turned around and surveyed the basement. Just below the ceiling was a long, narrow ground-level window. It opened up behind some shrubs near the front lawn. Kayla dragged a crate over to a spot beneath the window, stood on it, and cranked the window open.

"Erin! Jon! I'm locked in the basement!" she shouted as loudly as she could. She shouted again, and this time Erin heard her.

"What are you doing?" Erin asked, kneeling next to the basement window.

"I found the pack, but I got locked in," Kayla explained.

Erin gave her a funny look. "How?"

"I don't know how. The door just closed. Can you come inside and unlock it?"

"Just give me a minute," Erin said.

While she waited, Kayla set the flashlight on its side and started transferring her things from her Kate Spade bag into the pack. The middle compartment was more than big enough for all her clothes. Then she unzipped one of the side pockets for her cosmetics and noticed something inside. She reached in and felt something smooth and thin, like a piece of cardboard.

She pulled it out and aimed her flashlight at it.

Kayla started to shake as she saw an image of a skeletal knight emerging from a horrifying background. "I don't believe this," she murmured.

It was the Death Card. The same one she kept seeing in her dreams.

7

The light from the basement door opening startled Kayla.

"Hey—are you all right?" Erin asked, starting down the stairs.

Kayla quickly stuffed the tarot card back into the side pocket of the pack. "Yeah, I'm fine," she said, trying to sound calm. But she didn't *feel* calm. She felt weird. What was the tarot card doing in this old backpack? And what about the pack itself? Her father had taken all his things when he moved out. Which meant that the pack belonged to her mom.

So why did my mother, who hates anything connected to the occult, have a tarot card? Kayla asked herself. Is it as old as this pack?

"How did you get locked in?" Erin asked again.

Kayla shook her head. "Must have been a breeze coming in from the kitchen window or something." She made a quick, instinctive decision not to mention the Death Card to Erin or Jon until she knew more herself. Jon would only tell her she was nuts, and Erin might get even more nervous.

"So do you still really want to go through with this trip?" Erin asked. "I mean, are you sure you really know why we're going to begin with?"

"There's nothing about this that I'm sure about," Kayla admitted. "But all these dreams I've been having . . . I feel like there's something in them I'm meant to understand. And the only way I'll be able to do that is if I go to Deep Creek Lake."

Erin nodded. "It's just that I was thinking that if the Blair Witch evil really *is* in Deep Creek Lake, it could get pretty hairy."

"I know," Kayla said. "Look, if you want to bail, I'll totally understand. There's no reason for you to—"

"I'm not bailing," Erin told her. "I was there the night this whole thing started. Now I want to see it through."

The cousins gave each other a quick hug, then went back outside where Jon was finishing a cigarette. "Everyone got everything they need?" he asked.

"My stuff's all in the car," Erin said.

"And mine's all in here," Kayla said, setting her pack in the open trunk.

Jon pulled Kayla close for another kiss. "Now I have everything I need," he said so only she could hear.

Kayla kissed him back. "Then let's go," she said, and the three of them piled into the car.

✖✖

THEY'D BEEN DRIVING for hours. So far the scenery along Route 40 heading west toward Deep Creek Lake was an endless, boring stretch of highway. Erin was sleeping in the backseat.

"Hey, Kayla." Jon's voice was a whisper. "What if we ditch the whole witch thing and go north instead? This guy I know, Danny Alessio—his parents have a house up by Beaver Creek. The parents will be in D.C. this weekend, so he and his brother are getting a keg. It's going to be a total party."

"Are you kidding? My mother would kill me!"

"And she'd approve of you going to Deep Creek Lake?"

"I didn't say that." Kayla sighed.

"Well, your mother's away this weekend, so what she thinks doesn't matter. What do *you* want to do?"

Kayla debated silently. Jon had just given her a way out. She didn't have to go to Deep Creek Lake after all. The sick feeling in her stomach would go away.

Jon's hand circled her wrist. "C'mon, Kayla. We could have fun this weekend. I bet there'll even be someone up there Erin would like."

Kayla gave him a suspicious scowl. "Were you planning this all along?"

"Would I be driving on this butt-ugly road if I was? No, I was—and still am—all set to go tramping through the woods with you. But Danny called me about this party last night. And I can't help thinking it might be a better idea."

"It might." Kayla had to agree. Then again, a lot of the parties Jon went to seemed to end with some irate neighbor calling the police.

Jon's hand began to slide up and down Kayla's arm. "I've seen Danny's house. It's got a pool table, a hot tub, a swimming pool, and a wide-screen TV. It'd be like staying in a hotel. You'd forget all about this hokey witch—"

Would I? Kayla wondered. She knew she couldn't forget finding the tarot card. She still couldn't believe something from her dreams had appeared in her mother's old backpack. It seemed like some kind of proof to her—proof that those dreams were part of a puzzle that she had to solve. And until she did, she knew the dreams wouldn't stop. She had no choice. She had to find Deep Creek Lake.

Kayla closed her hand over Jon's. "The party sounds great," she told him. "And I'd love to go.

Really. But I can't. I feel like Deep Creek Lake is . . . calling me. And I need to find out why."

Jon shot her a look that was half contempt, half pity. "Okay," he said stiffly. "If that's what you want."

Kayla squeezed his hand. "Next weekend we'll do something you want to do."

The corners of his mouth turned up in a grin. "Be careful what you promise, girl. 'Cause I'll hold you to it."

Kayla was about to set some hasty limits on her promise when something hit the windshield with a loud *splat*.

"Oh, terrific," she muttered. "Just what we need when we're camping—rain!"

Splat! Splat!

Kayla peered through the windshield. "I've never seen such huge raindrops."

"Uh—Kayla," Jon said. He sounded uncharacteristically tense. "That's because it's not rain."

"What do you mean?"

"Check it out!"

And then Kayla realized that John was right. It wasn't rain hitting the windshield. They were driving into a cloud of slimy black bugs.

The bugs hit hard, leaving oily black splatters on the glass.

In the backseat Erin stirred. "What *are* those

things?" she asked in a drowsy voice. "Do you think they're some kind of beetle?"

"I don't care what they are. I just want them off my car," Jon snapped. He reached for the switch to turn on the windshield wipers, but Kayla stopped him.

"That'll just smear them," she said.

More bugs smacked against the windshield, each with a wet *thud*. The swarm got darker, thicker, completely surrounding the car.

Erin leaned forward in the backseat. "Whatever they are, they're incredibly gross."

"They're getting worse," Kayla said.

The bugs were hitting the windshield thick and fast. A heavy black slime oozed out of their smashed bodies.

Jon swore under his breath and leaned forward to peer through the bug-encrusted windshield. "This is ridiculous," he said. "There's, like, maybe two inches of clear windshield left."

"Try leaning on the horn," Erin told him in a panicked voice.

"What do you think that's going to do?" Kayla shrieked.

Jon didn't bother with the horn. His knuckles were white on the steering wheel. "I can't see anymore!" he cried. "Kayla, hang on. I can't drive!"

8

"Jon, pull the car over!" Kayla cried. "Get off the road!"

"I can't even see the road," Jon shot back. But he slowed down and rolled the Volvo to a stop on the shoulder of the highway.

"Eeeew," Kayla said as she stared at the windshield. It was nearly a solid mass of shiny, black bugs. Most of them were still half alive. Tiny, black, hair-like legs waved in the air as the black slime oozed from their bodies.

In the backseat Erin looked sick to her stomach. "I've never seen so many bugs," she murmured. "This is freaky."

"Where are they all coming from?" Jon asked. "I mean, will we lose them if we turn around?"

Kayla glanced behind them. The air was thick with the flying black insects. "Doesn't look that way. I think we're in the middle of it."

Jon shook his head and unlocked his door.

"What are you doing?" Kayla asked.

"I can't see out the windshield. I can't drive. We have to get them off," he said as he opened his door, stepped outside, and shut it quickly.

Kayla hesitated a moment. She knew it wasn't fair to make Jon deal with the bugs on his own. Especially when this whole trip was her idea. She carefully opened her door, then darted out of the car to join him.

Kayla willed herself not to scream. She could feel the bugs on every inch of exposed skin. They gave off a horrible stink. And they were sticking to her arms, her neck, fastening themselves in her hair. The best she could do was bat them away from her face.

Jon had the trunk open and was looking around inside. He pulled out two big water bottles and handed one to Kayla. "Let's start pouring water over the windshield," he said. "Maybe they'll just wash off."

Erin had now carefully stepped out of the car. She was holding a zippered sweatshirt over her head.

"I've got two canteens of water in my pack, too," she said, and reached in to grab them.

The water rinsed away the bugs, but the black slime remained on the glass.

Jon went back into the trunk and got out an ice scraper.

"You two get back inside," he said. "This will work."

Before they climbed into the car, the two cousins began to pull the bugs off each other. It seemed that the moment they got one of the slimy black creatures off, another took its place.

Kayla felt herself panicking. What if they never got rid of them?

"Ugh," Erin said as she pulled one out of Kayla's hair. "They're like flying leeches. This is so disgusting."

"We can't keep standing out here in the middle of them," Kayla said. "Jon, just clear enough space on the windshield so you can see. We'll find a gas station and hose the rest of the slime off."

"It's a plan," Jon agreed. He was at her side a few moments later. With both Jon and Erin working together, they got the bugs off Kayla, and she ducked into the car. Next Jon managed to get Erin bug-free. Then he peeled off his own bug-covered T-shirt and used it to scrape the insects from the rest of his body, and he, too, bolted inside.

Kayla was shaking as Jon started up the Volvo. Her heart was racing. Calm down and take slow, deep breaths, she told herself. The last thing she needed was a stress-induced asthma attack. She had them sometimes. Her mom said she used to get them when she was Kayla's age, too.

She felt Jon reach over and take her hand. "You okay?" he asked. "You're trembling."

"What *was* that?" Kayla asked. "I mean, I've been attacked by mosquitoes and flies and gnats and even a spider once, but that—that was almost unnatural," she finished in a quiet voice.

"It was a nightmare!" Erin declared.

"Well, don't worry about it. It's over now," Jon said, but Kayla could hear a tremor in his voice. Cool, in-control Jon was every bit as shaken as she was.

> **NOTE FROM CADE MERRILL:** *The bugs that Kayla described sound identical to the ones that Sharon described attacking Alison, although neither Kayla, Jon, nor Erin was bitten. Kayla showed me a map indicating the approximate area where they encountered the bugs. I have since checked with Garrett County's Department of Agriculture. There is no report of any insect infestation at that time. Neither is there any record of clouds of bugs that would match Kayla's description.*

><

NEARLY HALF AN hour later they were parked in a filling station and Jon was hosing down the car.

Kayla offered him some of the chips she'd just bought in the convenience store.

"No way," Jon told her. "I don't want to even think about food when I'm still washing off dead insects."

Kayla turned away from the gross sight to see the gas station attendant approaching them. He was about twenty-five, wearing greasy overalls and a Baltimore Orioles baseball cap. The name CAL was stitched across his breast pocket. He glanced over at the Volvo.

"What happened to your car?" he asked.

Jon shrugged. "We hit a lot of bugs out near all those farms," he explained.

Cal rubbed his forehead. "We don't normally see bugs like that around here. Where y'all headed?"

"Deep Creek Lake," Kayla answered. "Do you know how far it is?"

Cal snorted with laughter. "You only missed the turnoff by *twenty-five miles.*"

Jon looked at Kayla. "About twenty-five miles back is where we hit the bugs," he said. "I think we were a little distracted."

"I don't want to drive back into that swarm," Kayla said, shuddering.

"You don't have to," Cal told them. "There are a couple of ways to get to Deep Creek Lake. Just up ahead is a turnoff to a two-lane road. It's kinda curvy, but it cuts right back over to Route 40. Then you'll hit 219. Should be quicker than going back the way you came."

Erin returned from the convenience store with an ice cream cone. "What's going on?" she asked.

"Little detour. No big deal," Kayla informed her, and they all got back into the car.

A mile north of the gas station Jon turned onto the road Cal had told them about. They rode for about an hour, and then Kayla began to check her watch. Cal hadn't told them how far Route 40 was, but shouldn't they have hit it by now?

"What's the matter?" Jon said irritably. "You keep checking your watch."

"It's been more than an hour since we left the gas station," Kayla said. "We should have been on Route 40 a long time ago. I think we're on the wrong road."

"We're not on the wrong road," Jon told her.

"Cal said Route 40 to 219 was shorter than the way we came. And that only took us half an hour," she argued.

"What do you want me to do?" Jon asked.

Erin leaned in from the backseat. "Can we stop and ask for directions?"

Jon thought that was funny. "Where, Erin? We're in the middle of nowhere."

"He's got a point," Kayla said. Dense forest lined both sides of the road. Dusk was fading to darkness, and there were no lights anywhere.

"We're on the right road," Jon insisted. "The turnoff will be coming up soon. Why don't you two just go to sleep or something?"

Kayla was certain they were lost.

Then Kayla felt the car accelerating and noticed Jon's hands gripping the steering wheel more tightly. She looked over and saw the speedometer inching up. Great, she thought, Jon doesn't think we're lost, he just thinks he's driving too slow. They were now going seventy on a country road where the speed limit was forty-five.

"Jon, could you slow down?" Kayla asked.

Jon floored it. The speedometer hit seventy-five.

Eighty miles an hour.

Kayla glanced back at Erin. Her arms were straight out; her fingers were gripping the seat in front of her.

"Jon, you have to slow down! You're going to get us killed!" Kayla pleaded, but she looked at the road ahead of them and realized it was too late.

"Hold on!" Jon shouted as a deer darted across the road—directly in front of them.

"You're going to hit it!" Kayla shouted.

Jon slammed on the brakes. The screeching of the tires was deafening.

Kayla screamed as the car shot into a spin. She shut her eyes and waited for their lives to be over.

9

The Volvo spun once, twice, then hit the dirt on the side of the road. It finally came to an abrupt stop in the middle of the highway.

Kayla opened her eyes. The deer had moved on. "We're not dead?" she asked.

Jon was quiet.

Kayla turned around. "Erin, are you all right?" she asked. Erin barely managed a nod.

"I'm sorry," Jon said quietly.

"Why were you driving so fast?" Kayla asked. "You almost got us killed."

"I don't know." Jon ran a hand through his hair. "It felt like we'd been on the road all day. I was frustrated.

I just wanted to get there." He shrugged. "At least the car wasn't totaled."

Jon started up the car again and pulled it over to the shoulder. Kayla opened the glove compartment and pulled out the map of western Maryland that she'd put in before they left Frederick. While Jon got out to smoke a cigarette, Kayla traced the routes they'd driven. "I think I just figured out where we are," she said.

Erin sat forward, studied the map over Kayla's shoulder, and winced. "It looks like we're a long way from Deep Creek Lake."

"No kidding. We're totally on the wrong road." Kayla couldn't help feeling depressed. "I thought that by now we'd be at the lake with our tents up," she said wistfully, "eating those freeze-dried dinners Jon brought."

Jon got back in the car. "What's the verdict?" he asked in a grim tone.

"We're about two hours away," Kayla told him, and pointed to where they were on the map. "Somehow we got on this road, which took us south instead of west."

He leaned over and squinted. "How did *that* happen? I took the road that guy told me to take."

"I think his directions were off. Way off. We might as well keep going until it hits this highway. Then we'll go north until we're back on 40."

Jon shook his head. "I'm beginning to think this trip was a lousy idea," he muttered.

Kayla was feeling the same way, but she was determined to see it through. She had to. She folded the map and started to put it back into the glove compartment.

"Keep that out," Jon told her. "There's no way we're getting lost again."

∞∞∞

THEY DIDN'T GET LOST. But their two-hour car ride had turned into a five-and-a-half-hour slog, and it was after ten that night when they finally saw the sign welcoming them to Deep Creek Lake, population 2500.

"I don't think we should set up camp in the dark," Erin said quietly. "Can we just sleep in the car?"

Kayla glanced at Jon. She knew he'd been hoping for a romantic evening in the woods with her. It was what she'd wanted, too. But now they were all so worn out and frayed. . . .

"The car's okay with me," Jon said in a quiet voice.

"Me too," Kayla agreed.

Jon parked the car in a clearing just on the edge of town. Then he popped the trunk and got out their sleeping bags.

"Why don't you stretch out in the backseat, Erin?" Kayla suggested. "Jon and I can just put our seat backs down."

Jon didn't protest. He pushed the steering wheel as high as it would go, then lowered the back of the seat and turned on his side so that he faced Kayla.

"You okay?" he asked her.

"I guess. Sorry it was such a crazy trip getting here," Kayla said, knowing that it really wasn't her fault. She wondered if it was anyone's fault, or just a strange run of bad luck.

"Whatever." Jon leaned over and kissed her lightly on the lips. "Try and sleep," he said. Taking his own advice, he closed his eyes and started snoring lightly almost at once.

Kayla gazed out the window into the dark night.

"Are you sure you really know why we're going there to begin with?" Erin had asked her this afternoon. Kayla couldn't get the question out of her head. As the day had worn on, she'd asked herself the same thing over and over. Now they were finally in the town of Deep Creek Lake, and Kayla felt no closer to knowing.

The trip had gotten off to a rocky start. But tomorrow would be better, she told herself as she pulled the sleeping bag up to her chin and closed her eyes.

Kayla didn't know what time it was when she woke up. And at first she couldn't figure out what had woken her. Then she realized it was a sound. Footsteps outside the car.

"Jon?" Kayla whispered, but Jon was in a dead-to-the-world deep sleep, and she could hear Erin snoring in the back.

Kayla suddenly felt very alone. She turned her head slightly, toward the sound of the footsteps.

Across the road in the dim light of the moon stood a boy with shaggy blond hair. He was dressed in faded jeans and a Plague T-shirt. He was staring directly at her, a hauntingly familiar look on his face.

Was she dreaming again? Kayla shut her eyes for a moment, then opened them.

The boy was still there. He wasn't a dream figure. He was real. And now he was standing right up against the car.

BAM!

His fist pounded the window in front of her face.

Kayla wanted to wake Jon, but her voice was frozen in her throat, her body paralyzed with terror.

BAM!

His fist slammed against the window again. As if trying to shatter it.

What do you want? Kayla asked silently.

And then she realized exactly what it was that he wanted.

He wanted to get in.

PART IV:

Sharon and Gavin—Summer 1974, continued

*Based on taped interviews
with Sharon Maynard*

10

I stared into Gavin's dead, unseeing eyes.

The lights in the cabin suddenly went on, and I heard laughter behind me. The boys were howling, all of them: Carl Wagner, Stu Green, Tim Ferguson.

Gavin started to blink nervously and sat up in bed, rubbing his eyes. "What happened?" he asked. Then he looked up and saw me.

"Sharon?" he said. "Why are you dressed like that?"

I couldn't believe it. Gavin wasn't dead! And he'd recognized me, even in my witch costume. I didn't know what to say. "You sleep with your eyes open?" I managed, finally.

"Maybe, sometimes," Gavin said, sounding defensive. "But why . . . ?" Then he looked down and saw the chicken bones on his blanket. He started screaming and shaking them off.

"What are these?" he cried.

I thought Carl was going to wet his pants laughing. He came over and punched Gavin on the shoulder. "They were playing a joke on you, man," he said. "Sharon was pretending to be your favorite person. The Blair Witch."

Then the door of the cabin opened, and Marie walked in with Kathy, Carrie, and Carolyn. "Does anyone want to explain what's going on?" Marie asked, glaring straight at me.

"It's no big deal," Gavin said, sniffling a little. "They were trying to make me look stupid. I'm used to it."

It figures, I thought. Gavin manages to make himself look pathetic and us seem cruel, all at the same time.

"All right, let's go, girls," Marie said, her voice tight with anger. "And, Sharon, take off that ridiculous costume," she snapped.

"Come back real soon," Stu called as Marie escorted us out of the cabin.

Marie didn't wait until we got back to our bunk to clue us in about our punishment.

"Tomorrow, all the upper-level campers are going waterskiing. Except you three. You'll be in arts and crafts with the younger kids," she informed us.

"That's not fair! Those kids are eight years old," I protested.

"Well, maybe you can help them with their projects," Marie told me. "Who knows—maybe they'll want to make witch costumes."

><><

WHEN MY CABIN MATES and I walked into the arts and crafts room the next day, we saw a dozen little kids waiting for us. Each kid had an 8 x 11-inch piece of plywood in front of him or her. Scattered along the table were bowls filled with twigs, leaves, feathers, buttons, beads, keys, and plastic charms.

"Today we're going to make collages," Mrs. Gregory began. "You'll use the plywood as your canvas and glue things on to it. But first I want to introduce our special assistants who are sitting at the back table: Carrie, Carolyn, Sharon, and Kathy. If you need any help with your project, be sure and ask one of them."

A ceiling fan swirled slowly above us, but the small, crowded room was stiflingly hot. And Mrs. Gregory watched our every move. This is going to be a very long day, I thought.

Sure enough, it was Bore City. But finally two-thirty arrived. We were out of there.

Almost. "I want you all to leave your projects on the table at your places," Mrs. Gregory told the kids.

"Our helpers will apply a coat of varnish to your collages."

"Oh, great!" Carolyn moaned. "That'll take us forever."

Mrs. Gregory handed each of us an aerosol can. "Just spray the projects lightly and put them outside against the wall to dry. Then you're all dismissed." She frowned. "And I don't ever want to see you girls in here again."

"We're not in a hurry to see *you* again, either," Carrie mumbled as everyone else left. "What a waste of a day!"

"All because of that repulsive Gavin," Kathy said.

I sighed. I couldn't even stand thinking about that creep anymore. "Let's just forget about Gavin, okay? We've only got a couple of days left here."

"Hey, we can forget about Gavin, no sweat," Carrie said, shrugging. "But here's the real question: Will *he* forget about *you*?"

><

MARIE CAME BARGING into our cabin the next morning for the wake-up call. But today she didn't give us her usual "Rise and shine!" Instead, she said angrily, "Mrs. O'Connor wants to see you guys outside the arts and crafts room—right now!" She ordered us to get dressed quickly and follow her. We were totally confused, but we were all too sleepy to protest.

Mrs. O'Connor was the camp director. She was about forty, thick around the middle, and sharp-tongued. When we arrived at the arts and crafts room, she was standing outside with her arms folded across her chest. Mrs. Gregory stood beside her.

The camp director glared at us. "Which one of you wants to explain *this*?" she asked, gesturing to where we had left the kids' collages to dry.

The collages were gone. In their place, resting against the wall, were the strangest, ugliest little dolls I had ever seen. Each one was made of sticks and twigs bound together with twine.

"What are they?" Carolyn asked, wrinkling her nose.

"That's exactly what I was going to ask you," Mrs. O'Connor said.

"Uh, scarecrows?" Kathy guessed.

I drew closer to get a better look, my heart pounding. There was something strange—evil—about those stick figures.

I reached out a hand to touch one and jumped back quickly. I couldn't believe it.

Blood dripped from each creepy little doll, puddling on the ground beneath.

11

I stared at the macabre twig figures. I couldn't seem to look away, even though I wanted to.

"Gavin," I muttered. I didn't realize that Mrs. O'Connor was standing right behind me.

"Marie, please go get Gavin Burns," she said.

The counselor headed for the dining hall, then returned with Gavin a few minutes later.

"What's going on?" he asked. In the bright sunlight his skin looked almost transparent.

"Young man, are you responsible for this?" Mrs. O'Connor demanded. She pointed to the twig figures.

Gavin's face went even paler. "The witch!" he whispered. He turned to me. "She's here."

Suddenly I didn't feel creeped out anymore. I just felt mad. I was sick and tired of this witch thing. It was ruining my whole week at camp.

I marched straight up to Gavin and shoved him in his scrawny chest. "Just shut up about the witch, Gavin!"

Gavin stumbled backward, looking stricken.

"Sharon, Gavin, that's enough!" Mrs. O'Connor said sharply. "You're both on laundry duty for the remainder of the day. You will not participate in any of the scheduled activities." She waved Marie over. "Please show them what laundry duty entails. And the rest of you girls, clean up this mess!"

Gavin and I trailed after Marie. How did I get into this mess? I thought. It was all Gavin's fault. As usual.

"Hey, Sharon," Gavin whispered as we approached the laundry building. "This is pretty cool, huh?" He gave me an odd, twisted smile. "We're going to get to spend the whole day together. Just you and me. Alone."

∞

INSIDE THE LAUNDRY ROOM, Marie handed us each a plastic basket. "You have to collect the sheets and towels from all the cabins, then sort them here, and wash and dry them according to the instructions in the notebook on the table over there. Then you're going to fold everything neatly and return it to the cabins. Any questions?"

Gavin and I shook our heads.

Marie started out the door. "Try and be nice to each other, okay?" she called over her shoulder.

I gritted my teeth. Gavin was staring at me again. There's only one way to deal with him, I told myself. Ignore him. I wasn't going to say one word to that weirdo for the rest of our stay at camp.

After about twenty minutes of the silent treatment, Gavin seemed to get it. He stopped trying to talk to me. The two of us worked through the boys' cabins in complete silence.

Until we got to Cabin G.

Wordlessly we each took half the cabin. I got the side where Gavin slept. His day pack lay on the bed and fell to the floor when I impatiently pulled off the sheet. Something rolled out of the open outer pocket.

It was a pack of tarot cards. I picked them up. "You read the tarot?" I asked, frowning. This guy was even stranger than I'd thought. I'd never heard of any *guys* who were into tarot.

He shrugged. "Maybe."

I shook my head. "The Blair Witch, tarot cards, Plague, those horrible little stick figures you made—you're really into the dark stuff, aren't you? You actually think it's fun?"

"I didn't make those stick figures!" Gavin said indignantly. "I wouldn't mess with anything like that."

He came over and grabbed the tarot cards from my hand. Then he stuffed them back into his pack.

"What are those for, exactly?" I asked.

Gavin looked up at me. "You don't want to know."

"I do, actually," I said. It was true. I *was* a little curious. I'd heard you could tell the future with the tarot. But I'd never seen anyone do it.

"You *really* want to know?" he asked.

I shrugged. "Sure."

"Well, my uncle Bill works at the Burkittsville Historical Society. He pretty much runs the place. Anyway, I was there one day, just poking around, and I came across this old, dusty book called *The Blair Witch Cult*. It's seriously scary."

"Like, how?" I asked.

"The book tells about some of the things the Blair Witch is responsible for. Kids disappearing, rats and wolves being eaten alive—all kinds of weird stuff. Anyway, there was this cult that believed the witch's evil could be challenged by certain mystical rituals. And they thought that a certain combination of tarot cards could channel enough power to ward off her evil." He held up the cards.

"Sounds crazy," I said. But as I spoke, I felt that strange pressure on my neck again. I quickly reached up to my throat, but there was nothing there.

Gavin peered at me with his beady, watery eyes. "What's wrong?" he asked.

"N-nothing," I stammered, backing away. The pressure on my neck lessened.

Gavin shrugged and started flipping through the tarot cards until he came across one with a strange picture of a creepy skeleton carrying a scythe. Across the bottom, in big fancy letters, was the word DEATH. It sent a shiver down my spine.

Gavin held the card out to me.

"This is the most important card of all. If you meet the Blair Witch without it, you're doomed," he said. "And those stick figures outside the arts and crafts building, they're in the book, too. The cult considers them symbols of her evil. So she must be here, Sharon. You see?"

"Cut it out, Gavin," I said, looking toward the cabin door. "I don't want to talk about this anymore."

Gavin stepped toward me again. "Why not? You know, I'm kind of an expert on the Blair Witch. When you get near the Black Hills outside of my hometown, Burkittsville, you can actually feel her presence. I have the exact same feeling here."

I sighed. "Why would she come to Deep Creek Lake? What does she want with us?"

"You're making fun of me," Gavin said. "Just like everyone else. I'm telling you all this for your own good, Sharon. I *like* you. And I can help you."

Well, I don't like *you*, I wanted to say. Help me? What was it with this guy and all his creepy witch ideas? Why didn't he just leave me alone?

"I can prove to you that the witch exists," Gavin said, standing a little taller.

"Fine," I said, stuffing another set of sheets into my basket. "You do that."

"Tomorrow," Gavin said, in a low, dramatic tone. "You'll meet the witch tomorrow."

"Okay," I said, heading for the cabin door. I wanted to put as much distance between me and Gavin Burns as humanly possible.

"I can protect you," Gavin called after me. "I'm holding the Death Card."

NOTE FROM CADE MERRILL: *The book to which Gavin Burns refers is* The Blair Witch Cult. *Although the book purports to be a history of the Blair Witch and witchcraft in America, it is considered fiction.*

There are mentions in the book of a cult that used objects of ritual magic. However, I have never seen nor heard about any mention of tarot cards. Although Gavin examined the book almost thirty years ago, it's questionable whether he would have been able to get much information from it. Maybe he made some of the material up in order to impress Sharon.

I've found nothing in my research that supports tarot cards in general being used as some sort of magical protection. However, different decks portray the images of the tarot differently, and each deck has its own interpretation for the cards. Erin was correct when she told Kayla that the Death Card can indicate evil continuing beyond death.

12

Early the next morning twenty of us older campers and five counselors piled into two large vans and headed to the ranger station in Garrett State Forest. The trail we'd be taking was a full-day hike. We would start off a mile south of Deep Creek Lake.

I made sure to find a seat in the back of the van, as far as possible from Gavin Burns. I didn't even turn my head as I passed him on my way down the aisle. But I could feel him watching me.

A few minutes later, we arrived at the ranger station. We piled out of the vans and gathered in front of an athletic-looking counselor named Scott, who stood at the base of the trail.

"Listen up, guys!" he called. "Everyone pick a

partner. And don't turn this into a popularity contest, okay? The person you're standing next to is fine."

I winced as Gavin appeared out of nowhere and stood next to me.

"Stay close to your group's assigned counselor," Scott went on. "We'll be stopping often to examine plants and animal tracks and discuss the ecostructure of the area."

"Ecostructure?" I mumbled under my breath. Meeting a witch suddenly sounded like fun.

"There's a picnic area next to the lake where we'll be stopping for lunch. Any questions?" Scott asked. When there were none, he turned and started up the trail. "Onward!" he shouted.

We set off on the trail, which immediately started going uphill. I hadn't expected it to be so steep. I wondered if I was going to have trouble breathing again. Just concentrate on the hike, I told myself.

I tried to pick up my pace, but after a few minutes I started to huff and fall behind. It didn't help much to have Gavin right there beside me, either. I could hardly breathe with him so close to me.

"Very clever, Sharon," Gavin said. "Let everyone else go on ahead. Then it'll be easy to ditch."

I sat down on a rock, feeling a little dizzy. "Ditch?" I repeated, frowning.

"Sure," Gavin said. "We're going to find the Blair Witch, remember? Just like I promised."

"I don't think I can go anywhere right now," I protested.

"Of course you can," Gavin said, pulling me to my feet. "It's just up this way. We'll start with the bog."

"Why there?" I asked. I'd seen the bog detailed on the huge map that was hanging in the dining hall at the 4-H Center. The bog was next to the lake but hidden near the base.

"Instinct tells me that's where we'll find her," Gavin replied. His eyes were focused straight ahead, and his voice was grim. "Don't worry," he added. "I can protect you, remember? I have the card."

It seemed as if the area we were walking toward was completely dark. "It looks like night over there," I said, scrambling after Gavin. Even though I couldn't stand him, I didn't want to be left alone out there in the woods. I suddenly felt like some kind of . . . well, target. I couldn't shake this growing feeling of dread.

To the east, Metal Mountain definitely seemed to block out the sun. Or was it the tall trees that surrounded the area? I couldn't tell. I decided I was so hungry I was starting to see things. "I'm hungry," I announced.

Gavin sighed. "There's an apple in the top right pocket of my pack," he said, coming to a stop. "Reach in and take it."

I gratefully grabbed the apple and took a bite.

"C'mon, we haven't got all day," Gavin said. He was really getting impatient now.

"Okay, okay," I answered. As I scrambled to catch up, I dropped the apple on the ground. I reached down to retrieve it, then drew back in horror. The apple seemed to have disappeared into the earth!

"Did you see that?" I asked Gavin.

He nodded. "We're near the bog, all right. Stick very, very close to me, okay?"

"Oh, sure," I said. "I feel so safe."

Gavin ignored me as the two of us walked deeper into the darkness. There weren't any birds singing in this part of the woods. Just something making a strange clicking sound. Frogs? I wondered nervously.

"Shhhhh!" Gavin put his finger to his lips. The sound suddenly stopped, and there was an eerie silence. Then horrid crunching sounds started echoing through the woods, as though we were stepping on bones.

"What is that?" I asked, drawing closer to Gavin in spite of myself.

"I don't know," he said. He sounded scared now.

Suddenly I noticed a thick white mist ahead of us covering the bog. There was definitely something strange about it. Something *wrong*. "Gavin, forget about the witch," I whispered. "We're going back."

Gavin shook his head. "Just a little farther," he said. "I want you to have your proof."

"I don't care, okay?" I told him. "I just want to get out of here."

"No," Gavin said. "We have to go through with this."

"I believe you, okay?" I practically screamed. "The Blair Witch is real!"

But Gavin just kept walking. The mist was thick, and it was almost impossible to see now. Gavin stumbled over a fallen tree, and I fell right on top of him.

He felt cold and clammy. "Ughhh," I said, pushing myself off.

Then I saw that Gavin's backpack had opened. Everything inside, including the tarot cards, lay scattered all around us on the ground.

Gavin scrambled to his feet and frantically began retrieving his gear.

I tried to stand up, too—and felt a sharp burning in my right ankle. "Ow!" I cried, sitting down again. "I think I twisted my ankle."

"Terrific," Gavin said. "That's just what we need."

"Hey, I fell over *you*, " I pointed out.

Suddenly the eerie silence around us was broken by a painful, high-pitched moan, as if a child were in pain.

We heard the awful sound again. Louder this time.

Screeching, crying.

A child gasping for breath?

Instinctively my hand went to my throat. I couldn't help thinking of what had happened to me.

"It's the witch!" Gavin said softly. He turned around and raced off in the opposite direction, deeper into the bog.

"Gavin, wait!" I cried.

I didn't want to be alone in this mist. My ankle was throbbing, but I knew I had to get moving. I had to get out of there. I pressed my hands against the ground, to push myself up—and touched something smooth. I looked down and saw the unmistakable drawing of a skeletal figure. Gavin's Death Card!

"Gavin, stop!" I cried, grabbing the card and forcing myself to my feet.

The moaning changed. Now it sounded like a woman wailing. My heart started to race.

"Gavin!" I screamed one last time. Through the thick mist I could barely see his silhouette about twenty yards ahead.

"Sharon, help! I can't move," Gavin shouted. "I'm stuck in the bog—I can't get out!"

I tried to move toward him, but I was stuck, too. I couldn't move a muscle. And all around me I could feel the evil that Gavin had talked about. It was *real*. And it wanted to kill us both.

"Sharon, please!" Gavin begged.

I fought to move. It felt as though my entire body were paralyzed. I couldn't even close my eyes. I could only stand, helplessly, watching Gavin a short distance away.

The moaning grew louder, closer.

I watched in horror as the mist turned into a heavy fog—and a faint shape rose out of the vapors. It looked like a woman in a cloak. Then it seemed to shimmer and fade.

"Oh, my God!" Gavin screamed. "It's *her*! I told you!"

I was about to breathe a sigh of relief as the fog woman began to dissolve. But then I saw the fog swirl into a funnel, winding itself into a rope of dark mist.

"Shaaaaaron!"

Now the rope was wrapping itself around Gavin's neck. I could see his eyes bulge as he reached for his throat. Terrible choking sounds escaped from his mouth.

I watched the dark rope tighten. And tighten.

Gavin gave one last horrible choking scream—before his head flew from his body.

13

I covered my eyes and wept in horror—and pure terror. Then I realized I'd moved my arms—the paralysis was gone! So was Gavin—and the killer. Had it been the witch? And if so, why had she spared me? I didn't know. And I didn't care.

I turned and ran away from the bog and the terrible scene I had witnessed. My ankle felt as though it were on fire, but I ignored it. I could bear the pain as long as I got away from there. My feet bounced over the spongy earth, propelling me over the fallen logs. I was limping badly, but I forced my body to move faster. The only thing that mattered was putting as much distance as possible between me and the Blair Witch. And poor, dead Gavin.

I was completely winded and sobbing hysterically when I finally stumbled back to the 4-H group. I hardly noticed the presence of the park rangers who'd apparently been called when Gavin and I were discovered missing.

Mike was the first one to spot me. "What happened?" he cried, rushing over. "Where's Gavin?"

I pointed back in the direction of the bog and tried to speak, but the words caught in my throat.

Mike put a hand on my shoulder. "Try and calm down," he told me.

I kept pointing through the trees, trying to tell him about the bog, about Gavin, but I couldn't seem to get the words out.

"Here." One of the park rangers handed me a cup of water. "Drink this and take a few nice deep breaths. Then try to tell us what happened, okay?"

I nodded. The water helped, and so did the deep breathing. I began to feel a little calmer. "Gavin and I went off," I began. "To the bog. And Gavin got stuck in the swamp. And then the—" I wrestled with the next word in my mind. What I wanted to say was "witch."

"Bear," I said aloud.

"A *bear* got him?" The ranger sounded doubtful.

"A black bear," I said. What was wrong with me? I felt possessed, as if someone else were putting words in my mouth, talking through me. It was as if I had no control over what I said next. "It was awful. Gavin's dead."

"Get your rifles," one of the park rangers told the others.

I was dimly aware of all the kids staring at me. Did they believe the bear story? Probably. Who would believe that Gavin and I had actually encountered the Blair Witch, and that she had killed him?

The next few hours were a blur. More park rangers were called in, all carrying rifles, and they headed to the bog. No one made me explain why Gavin and I had sneaked away in the first place. At least, not yet. When they did, I would lie. I would never mention anything about the evil. Never utter the words *Blair Witch*.

I pushed my hand into the back pocket of my jeans and fingered the tarot card Gavin had left behind.

I stared at the word DEATH printed across the bottom of the card. Had I been holding the one thing that could have saved his life? Or had the card simply foretold Gavin's fate?

I will never know.

PART V:

Plague

Based on taped interviews with Kayla Maynard,
Erin Daley, and Deep Creek Lake
Park Ranger William Mallory

14

Kayla shrank back from the window. It was shuddering under the boy's blows. He raised his fist for a last blow, the one that would finally shatter the glass, and Kayla screamed.

"Calm down, miss!" said a stern voice outside the car. "I just want to ask you kids a few questions."

Kayla blinked a few times and realized it was light outside. Morning. A cop was standing outside her window. Kayla could see that he'd been pounding his fist against the glass, trying to wake them.

But where did the boy go? she wondered. That wasn't a dream. He was so real, and so, so . . . Kayla couldn't put her finger on it.

Kayla started to roll her window down. Beside her

Jon sat up with a start. "What's going on?" he mumbled as he saw the cop.

The cop stuck his head in through the open window. "I was going to ask you the same question. What are you all doing out here? We don't encourage people to sleep in their cars on the side of the road."

Erin sat up in the backseat, squinted, and gave a sleepy, "Huh?"

"Sorry, Officer," Jon said quickly. "We were supposed to get to Deep Creek Lake yesterday afternoon, but we had a few mishaps along the way and didn't arrive until after ten. We didn't want to set up camp in the dark."

The cop's eyes narrowed. "What kind of mishaps?"

"We got lost twice," Jon explained.

"And what campground are you headed to?" the officer wanted to know.

"We're not," Kayla answered. "We're going off trail."

"Well, in that case you're going to have to follow me to the park ranger," the cop told her. "If you're not staying in a campground, we want you to fill out a form telling us where you intend to go. That way, if something happens to you, we'll know where to look."

"If something happens to us?" Erin echoed.

"A lot of people go off into the woods without knowing the first thing about it," the cop explained in a dry tone. "You'd be amazed at how many week-end warriors the park rangers have to bail out."

Jon rolled up the window and started the Volvo. "Great," he muttered. "Just how I wanted to start my morning. Playing Follow the Cop. We're never going to get there at this rate."

"Maybe it's a good idea to register," Erin said.

Jon glared at her in the rearview mirror but followed the police car. Twenty minutes later they pulled up behind the officer's car in front of the park ranger's headquarters, a small brick building in the middle of town. Jon held the front door open for Kayla and Erin, a sour expression on his face.

The cop led the way into the office, where a ranger whose nametag read W. MALLORY sat behind the counter.

"These kids are going off trail," the cop explained. "I wanted them to check in with you first."

Mallory looked at the three teens with a puzzled expression. "What are you going off trail for? We have terrific campgrounds all along the lake."

"We're going on a witch hunt," Jon answered.

"Pardon?" Mallory said.

"He's just kidding." Kayla jumped in quickly. "We're headed to the bog." She figured there was no harm in telling the truth. After all, what if something *did* happen to them there?

"The bog? Why would anyone except a botanist

want to go to the bog? There's nothing there except a lot of plant life and soggy ground that's treacherous if you try to cross it. Plus bogs attract snakes and breeding mosquitoes." He pulled a complimentary map from under the counter. "However, there are a lot of other areas I'd be glad to recommend."

"Actually, we are interested in botany," Kayla lied. "The three of us are working on a summer project about the . . ."

". . . the ecostructure of the area," Erin filled in.

The ranger shook his head. "I can't legally prevent you from going out there. But if there's any way I can change your minds . . ."

Kayla shook her head and smiled.

Mallory sighed and handed them each a form. "Well, then, fill these out," he told them.

As Kayla, Jon, and Erin wrote out their names, addresses, and phone numbers and agreed not to hold the park liable for any mishaps, the ranger took out a yellow marker and began highlighting trails on a topographic map. Kayla noticed he was highlighting a hiking trail that looked as though it started a few miles south of the bog.

"What about the fire road that takes you there?" she asked.

"Oh, that was washed out this winter with the storms," Mallory told her. "Hasn't been cleared yet. You'll have to hike up," he explained.

"Perfect," Jon muttered. "This just gets better and better."

"How far is it?" Kayla asked the ranger.

"About two miles. You'll start here." Mallory drew an X across a guard booth next to a parking lot. "Then head on up this way." He continued to highlight.

"There's no shorter way?" Jon asked.

"No, but it's a pretty hike. You can take a rest at this picnic area beside the lake." He drew another circle. "It's pretty run-down. The Forest Service no longer maintains it, but it's probably the only real clearing where you can pitch a tent. The bog's right over here." Mallory put his final mark on the map and handed it to Jon. "Just be real careful, okay?"

"We'll be fine," Kayla promised, starting for the door. "Thanks for your help."

Erin turned back to the ranger. "Has anything dangerous ever happened in that bog?"

Mallory shrugged. "Not recently," he replied. "There was an incident in the early seventies. A young man had a run-in with a bear, I believe. Beats me what a bear was doing down in the bog. They generally stick to the higher elevations."

"What happened to the guy?" Kayla asked.

Mallory gave her a grim smile. "You don't want to know."

✕

JON STRODE SWIFTLY across the parking lot, as if trying to put distance between himself and Kayla and Erin.

Kayla hurried to catch up with him. "Why did you tell the ranger we were going witch hunting?" she demanded.

"Isn't that what we're doing?"

"What's with you this morning?" Kayla asked. "You've been in a rotten mood ever since you woke up."

"Maybe I don't like waking up to a cop at the window," Jon said. "Maybe I had my fill of insects yesterday. And maybe it just feels like everything about this trip has been wrong from the start. You know, the more I think about it, the more I wish I'd gone to Danny's."

And the more *I'm* wishing you'd gone to Danny's, Kayla answered silently. "Look," she said, "you don't have to come with us. You can just drop us off at the trailhead, and—"

"And what, Kayla? I'm not going to let you two go off by yourselves. You've never been hiking before in your life."

Kayla and Jon glared at each other while Erin got back into the car. "Will one of you just make a decision?" she asked.

"We're going to check out the bog," Kayla stated.

"Oh, goody," Jon said.

Kayla decided to ignore that. "The Deep Creek

Lake Project is officially starting now," she told Erin. "We should get into documentary mode." She took her video camera out of the back of the car and started taping.

"We are now at the Deep Creek Lake Ranger Station," Kayla began. She focused on Jon first, knowing it would annoy him and not caring. "Jon Prellar is holding the map provided to us by Ranger William Mallory. Tell me, Jon, how do you feel as we are about to enter Garrett State Forest?"

Jon crossed his arms and glowered at the camera. "I'd rather be at Danny's party. Any other redundant questions?"

"Jon!"

"Well, it's true," he said. "This place isn't 'calling' anyone. We could drive up to Beaver Creek now and have a good Saturday night." He leaned toward Kayla and spoke in a whisper, "We could go skinny-dipping in the moonlight. . . ."

Kayla pushed him away. "Let's just finish what we started. We made it this far."

"Barely," he grumbled. He reached into his shirt pocket and pulled out his cigarettes and lighter.

"No smoking on camera," Kayla told him.

"Why not?" he asked. "We're outside."

"Because it will set a bad example for all the young filmmakers who will one day watch this documentary," Kayla told him in a fake-prim tone. "Besides," she added more honestly, "you know it aggravates my asthma."

John rolled his eyes but put the cigarette pack in his pocket. The lighter fell to the ground. "Okay," he said, "if I can't smoke, I get to hold the camera."

Kayla gave him the camera, then picked up the lighter from the ground and put it in her pocket while Jon focused the camera on Erin. "So, Erin," he said, "how do you feel about this insane trek into a mosquito-infested bog?"

"A little spooked, I guess."

"And why is that?" Jon asked in his best TV-newscaster voice.

"I don't know." Erin shrugged. "Things have been kind of weird ever since we started this trip."

"My point exactly." Jon glanced meaningfully at Kayla.

"But they'll be fine," Kayla said forcefully. "Everything is going to be fine."

"Well, now you have it, ladies and gentlemen. The official word on this trip. Everything is going to be fine. Remember that." Jon shut the camera off and handed it to Kayla. "Let's go already." He sounded disgusted.

They drove in silence until Jon turned the car onto a road marked with the sign for Garrett State Forest. Up ahead was the guard booth and just beyond that, the parking lot. Kayla squinted.

"Who is that?" She pointed at the guard booth.

"Where?" Jon asked.

"There." Kayla kept pointing. "That's the same— oh, my God, that's the guy who—" But she couldn't finish. She just pointed, her eyes wide with fear.

Standing in the guard booth, staring directly at her, was the boy in the Plague T-shirt. The one from her dreams who'd pounded on her window last night.

And this time he was real.

15

"Th-that guy!" Kayla was stammering. "Last night. When you and Erin were sleeping. H-he came up to my window. He was pounding on it—"

"Kayla." Jon had stopped the car. He was looking at her with concern. "What guy? Who are you talking about?"

Kayla pointed toward the guard booth.

But the boy in the Plague T-shirt was gone.

No one was there.

Kayla looked around. "I just saw him! He was standing—" She stopped talking. What she was saying sounded crazy. Even to her.

"Kayla, are you okay?" Erin asked. "There's no one there."

Kayla rubbed her eyes. "Well, I thought I saw someone," she said, knowing it sounded lame.

"And there was someone pounding on the car window last night?" Jon asked.

"I think so," Kayla answered in small voice.

"Why didn't you wake me?"

"I wanted to. I was too scared," she answered. "I don't know. Maybe it was a dream," she admitted.

Jon reached across and ruffled her hair. "You and your dreams," he said, his voice gentler than it had been all morning.

He drove past the empty guardhouse, then parked in the lot. There was only one other car there. "Popular spot," he noted. "Maybe everyone else was scared away by Ghost Boy."

"I'm going to get more water," Erin said, and grabbed the canteens and water bottles they'd emptied the day before to clean the bugs off the windshield. Jon put on his baseball cap, then headed for the public bathrooms on the edge of the lot.

Kayla got out of the car and watched them walk away. She knew they'd be back in a matter of minutes, so why did she feel so scared and alone? Her stomach was in knots. She hated the edgy, nervous way she felt, but she was *certain* that the boy from her dreams had been in the guard booth. Could he really be . . . Gavin? She looked all around her, wondering where he'd gone, wondering who he was,

what he wanted. And then she heard footsteps behind her.

Kayla jumped, but it was just Jon.

He put an arm around her. "Look at you," he said
gently. "You're all freaked out. What's wrong? You
don't actually believe you're going to find a witch,
do you?"

Kayla pulled away from him and bit back an angry retort. Jon had no right to be so condescending.
But the day had already gotten off to a lousy start,
and she wanted things to get better, not worse. She
couldn't afford to pick a fight.

"There's nothing wrong with me," she told Jon in
as calm a voice as she could manage.

She'd concentrate on taping and stop worrying
about Jon *and* the strange boy from her dreams. She
pulled the camcorder's strap over her head and
turned the camera on Erin, who had just returned
from the bathroom. "And here's Erin, making sure
we have plenty of water," Kayla said in a deter-
minedly cheerful voice.

Erin made a face at the camera, stuffed a canteen
into Kayla's pack, and handed Jon the water bottles.

"The trail starts over here." Kayla pointed to a dirt
path between two large rocks.

Jon locked up the car, and the three of them
shouldered their packs and started up the trail. Kayla
shot trees and ferns and moss for a while but

couldn't help noticing that something was bothering her cousin. "What's wrong, Erin?" she asked.

Erin shook her head. "Nothing."

"Erin, I've known you since you were a baby. I can tell when you're lying."

"It's what I said before. All this stuff is happening. It's weird." Erin put her hands over her face. "Do you have to film this?"

"Just keep talking," Kayla told her.

"Well, the parking lot was practically empty. That seemed strange. Then there were those bugs, and we got on the wrong road twice. And now you've seen a boy that neither one of us has seen. Also twice. Plus the ranger trying to warn us off. What if there *is* some kind of evil around here?"

"And what if it's all Kayla's imagination?" Jon chimed in.

"I didn't imagine those bugs yesterday," Kayla pointed out.

"Not those," Jon agreed. "But I can't help thinking that it's crazy to be hauling a seventy-pound pack up a trail, all because you've got some delusions about a witch and a boy who doesn't exist!"

Kayla had heard enough. "I'm not going to waste my time and energy fighting. If either one of you is uncomfortable, you can go back to the car. I'll come down as soon as I've checked out the bog."

"No, I want to go with you," Erin said at once. "I

just wanted to make sure I wasn't the only one who felt this way."

"Trust me, you're not," Jon said.

Kayla aimed the camera at him, but with a lightning-quick move he reached over and grabbed it out of her hand.

"Hey!" Kayla shouted, but Jon ignored her. He turned his baseball cap backward on his head and put the camera up to his eye. He smirked and started narrating, "It's Saturday afternoon. We've been wandering for weeks now. We have no food, no water. But we're having so much fun."

Kayla tried to grab the camera, but Jon kept it out of reach. "Jon, you jerk, give it back!"

"As you can see, Kayla's totally lost it," he continued. "We've decided to eat each other if we don't get food soon. If you find this tape, please send help."

Kayla gave up trying to get the camera back, but she did reach into Jon's pocket and grab Mallory's map. "I'm taking this," she said.

Jon shrugged. "Fine with me. Do whatever you want. Because personally, I just don't care."

"C'mon, Erin, let's go," Kayla said, and started marching forward. She only glanced back once to see if Jon was following. He wasn't.

"What's the matter with *you*?" she called.

"I'm heading back to the car!" he shouted.

"What do you mean, back to the car?" Kayla exploded. "You're going to desert us?"

Jon just shrugged again. Then he turned around and headed for the parking lot.

Kayla threw up her hands. "Fine!" she said. "Be that way."

"Do you think he'll take off and go to that party?" Erin asked, sounding worried.

"No, he'll just sulk for a while," Kayla predicted. "He's mad because he isn't getting all the action he expected on this trip. But he'd never leave us stranded. You'll see. He'll catch up with us later."

Kayla glanced at the map. "We've got a ways to go before we hit the bog," she said. "We'd better move it."

The two cousins hiked uphill for what seemed like forever. Even though they were walking beneath a canopy of leaves, the heat was intense. The afternoon had turned humid, and the hike was steep and strenuous. Walking uphill, the two miles to the lake felt like ten.

Kayla knew she ought to use her inhaler before she wound up having an asthma attack, but she didn't want to take off her pack and root around for it. Instead, she glanced at her watch and pulled the map out of her back pocket.

"I'm guessing that we're here," she said, pointing to a spot on the map that looked about three-quarters of the way from the parking lot to the bog. "Let's go a little farther and then take a break. That should give Jon a chance to catch up."

"Sounds good," Erin said. "I could definitely use a break."

They rounded a bend in the trail and groaned. The stretch of trail ahead of them rose even more steeply. "How come Mallory didn't warn us we'd be walking at a ninety-degree angle?" Erin grumbled.

Kayla shrugged and studied the map. "Well, all the little elevation lines on the map kind of hint at that."

"Kind of hint?" Erin studied the map. "Kayla, this trail is nearly straight uphill!"

"Just for a little ways," Kayla said. "Come on."

But ten minutes later both girls were breathing hard and soaked in sweat.

"Let's just stop here. I'm dying," Kayla panted, and collapsed onto the ground. She pulled the backpack off her shoulders. It was definitely time to use her inhaler. She unzipped one of the smaller pockets on the pack and began rummaging through it. Not there. She tried another pocket. "That's weird," she said.

"What?" Erin asked. She untied the red bandanna from her neck and wiped the sweat from her forehead.

"My inhaler," Kayla said. "I swear, I put it in one of these little outer pockets, and now I can't find it."

"Do you want to me look?" Erin asked.

Kayla shook her head and searched again. This time she also checked out the main compartment of the pack and even the pockets of her shorts. *Nada*.

"You don't have your inhaler?" Erin asked.

"It's no biggie," Kayla said. "My asthma's been really mild these last few months. The inhaler is more insurance than necessity."

"Are you sure?"

"I'll just drink some water," Kayla said. "I'll be fine." But the truth was, she was feeling a little panicky. It had been years since she'd gone anywhere without an inhaler. What had happened to it? *I must have dropped it in the basement when I was transferring stuff out of my tote,* she decided.

Kayla pulled out her canteen, unscrewed the top, and lifted it to her mouth. The cool water would feel so good sliding down her parched throat.

"Ugggh!" she cried as she realized it wasn't cool and it wasn't water. It was warm and had a horrid metallic taste. Kayla gagged and spit out the liquid.

"What's wrong?" Erin asked.

Kayla couldn't answer. She was on her hands and knees, gagging. A brownish-red liquid dripped down her chin.

She grabbed a bandanna from her pack, then wiped off her tongue and chin. "What's in here?" she gasped. She turned the canteen upside down. Thick reddish-brown blood pooled on the ground in front of her.

16

Erin backed away from Kayla. Her eyes were on the pool of brownish-red liquid that had come from Kayla's canteen. Her voice shook as she said, "What is it?"

Kayla wiped her mouth again and peered at the puddle on the ground. She reached toward it.

"Don't!" Erin warned. "We don't know what it is!"

"It looks like blood," Kayla said. "But it tasted like, well, I don't even *know* what it tasted like. What's in your canteen?"

Erin stared at the canteen in her hand as if it might bite her. Then she unscrewed the top and poured a little on the ground.

"Oh, gross!" Erin yelled when she saw it, too.

"Kayla, I swear, I filled these with water. I don't know how—"

"Do we have any other water?" Kayla asked.

Erin shook her head. "Jon has the other water bottles with him," she explained, "and the food."

"All of it?"

Erin nodded. "Back at your house, when you were down in the basement, we organized the packs. The food and water were the heaviest, so we put them in Jon's pack. You and I are carrying the tent, the sleeping bags, towels, and flashlights."

"Great. Jon's got all the water."

"You said he'd catch up with us," Erin reminded her. "Why don't we just wait for him?"

Kayla debated silently for a moment before answering, "Okay. I'm sure he'll be here soon." She hoped what she'd just said was true. But she was worried. And she didn't want Erin to know it.

They moved away from the brownish-red puddle on the ground and leaned their packs against some large stones on the side of the trail. Kayla sat on one of the rocks. Erin stood in front of her, shifting her weight from one foot to another.

"Now what?" Kayla asked.

Erin stopped shifting. "Do you think we should backtrack? That way we'll run into Jon and get the water sooner," she said.

Kayla studied her cousin's face. "You're scared, aren't you?"

Erin gave an overly casual shrug. "I'm okay without the food," she said. "But going without water in this heat—it's a really bad idea. I mean, dehydration is no joke. It can speed up your heart rate, give you muscle cramps, and make you weak and dizzy. Eventually you get really confused and lose consciousness."

"Thank you very much. That's something to look forward to."

"I'm not saying it will get that bad," Erin told her. "But I think it's a good idea to find Jon and the rest of our water."

"Considering we don't have water, we should probably let Jon find us," Kayla said. "You and I shouldn't be pushing it. Besides, we'll be easier to find if we stay in one place."

Erin sat on the ground next to Kayla. "True. That's always what they tell you to do if you're lost in the wilderness. So how long do we wait?"

Kayla didn't know the answer to that one. Fifteen minutes? An hour? Even though the sun was still bright, the afternoon shadows made it feel later than it was. And what if Jon didn't show up? What if he *had* gone back and taken the car? What if—?

"Half an hour. If he isn't here by then, we'll go on ahead," Kayla said, realizing that she had to take charge. Erin might have more outdoors experience, but Kayla was older. Besides, she was the one who was supposed to know Jon. She consulted the topographic map. "We're a lot closer to the lake than we are to the parking lot. We can get water there."

Erin wrinkled her nose. "The lake water may not be drinkable. It may have bacteria and stuff in it."

"I'll take bacteria over dehydration," Kayla said. She wiped away a bead of sweat that was sliding down to her elbow. "I can't believe I ever thought this trip was a good idea."

It seemed an even worse idea half an hour later when Jon still hadn't shown up. Kayla looked at her watch and got to her feet. She cupped her hands on either side of her mouth and called out, "Jon! Jon! Where are you?" Erin stood up and joined her, but no one answered their calls.

"We should have stuck together," Erin said.

"Too late to change things now," Kayla said. "Listen, I'm dying of thirst. Let's get to the lake."

Again they started to hike the steep trail. Erin walked with her eyes down and gave monosyllabic answers whenever Kayla tried to make conversation. Kayla wondered if her cousin was angry at her or just too hot and tired to talk.

Suddenly Erin's eyes lit up and she whirled around. "I hear someone!" she said.

Kayla turned around and listened.

"You're right," she said. "That sounded like footsteps. Jon, is that you? Jon!"

"We're over here!" Erin shouted.

They listened again. The footsteps died out. The woods were still.

Erin shot Kayla a panicked look.

"Maybe it was just an animal," Kayla said. "Come on, let's get to that lake."

They started walking again. And again the distinct sound of footsteps followed them. This time Kayla and Erin both turned around.

A high-pitched voice wailed, "Hello! Hellooo . . ."

Kayla shook her head. She was losing patience fast. "Very funny!" she called out, certain that Jon was having a good time busting them. "Come on, Jon. Stop with the jokes and get over here! We need the water!"

The footsteps grew louder, but there was still no Jon. Kayla stopped smiling.

"What if it's not Jon?" Erin asked in a small voice.

"It's him," Kayla said. She wasn't even going to consider the possibility that Erin might be right. "But he's being a jerk. So let's just keep going. We're almost at the lake."

Kayla felt herself stumbling as she pushed up the steep trail. Was it possible that her backpack had somehow doubled its weight? She was hot and tired and so thirsty that her throat was parched.

Kayla blinked as she heard something that sounded

like heavy-metal music playing nearby. "What is that?" she asked, hoping that Erin heard it, too.

"Music," Erin replied flatly.

"I *know* it's music. But where's it coming from?" Kayla looked around and realized the air around them had grown misty.

"Forget the music. Where did all this fog come from?" Erin wondered. "Maybe we're getting close to the water."

Kayla was still looking around her, trying to find the source of the music. It sounded like old heavy metal, the kind of thing they played at a seventies theme party.

"So you think you can escape the Dark?
Don't you know, it comes for us all in the end. . . ."

Kayla shuddered. The lyrics gave her the creeps. "Do you know who that band is?" she asked Erin.

"No, never heard 'em." Erin sounded distracted.

Then Kayla heard a man's voice say, "Carl, turn off that transistor radio and put it away!" The music stopped.

"Hello," Kayla called out. "Is anyone there?" She turned to her cousin. "Erin, did you hear that?"

But Erin was facing west, jumping up and down with excitement. "Kayla, look!" Erin pointed ahead of her. The fog was thinning. Kayla could see a clearing and, beyond it, sunlight sparkling off the lake.

We're saved! Kayla thought. Now they would have clean water to drink—and according to the map, it was only a short distance north from the lake to the bog.

Hurriedly she and Erin stumbled through the trees and came to the picnic area that the park ranger had told them about. Only it wasn't run-down the way he said it would be. The wooden picnic tables seemed polished and new, and there was none of the usual litter or debris. In fact, it looked as though no one had ever used the site before.

Kayla noticed something in the dirt underneath one of the tables. She bent down to get a closer look—and pulled out a large black cassette.

"What is that? A videotape?" Erin asked.

"That's what I thought it was," Kayla admitted. "But I think it might be music. My dad told me that when cassette tapes first came out in the seventies, there were also these larger-format tapes called eight-tracks. And everyone used to talk about how eight-tracks would win out and cassettes would disappear. But it didn't happen."

"Pretty clunky. Who's the band?"

Kayla turned over the cassette and saw a label on the other side. The name on it made her feel sick.

"Plague."

PART VI:

Jon

*Based on videotape footage taken
by Jon Prellar, June 29, 1999*

NOTE FROM CADE MERRILL: *Kayla's camcorder was recovered by the police in the investigation that followed their trip to Deep Creek Lake. I asked to be given access to the tape once the police were done with it, and was recently allowed to view it.*

The initial scenes on the tape are those referred to in Kayla's sections of the file: the pretrip interviews, and the bit that was shot in the parking lot before they set off on the trail. The rest of the tape was shot by Jon. I've tried to re-create what follows on the tape in this next section of the file.

17

"Okay, Jon Prellar here, left all alone while Kayla and Erin set off in pursuit of a witch. Boo-hoo."

The camera pans, and the guardhouse can be seen in the distance. Jon seems to be heading back toward the parking lot.

"I told them I'm going back to the car, to sound like I'm going off to Danny Alessio's place. Which would probably be the smart thing to do. But—"

The camera swings around again, and now Jon is back on the trail, heading uphill—

"—that was a lie, and Kayla knows it. I can't leave them here. Especially since I've got all of the food and most of the water. But hey, sometimes I just can't re-sist messing with Kayla's head. Especially when she deserves it for getting all three of us caught up in a wild-goose chase. I still can't believe she's got us heading for a mosquito-infested bog to hunt for a witch! So I'm going to sit down on this rock here—"

The camera zooms in on a large, flat white boulder.

"—and give Kayla and Erin a head start before I catch up with them."

At this point the camera starts zooming in and out on assorted plants and shrubs. The scene narrows and goes wide.

"Cool, a slow-time feature. I didn't know this camera could do that. I just might have to buy me my own camcorder. Sundance Festival, here I come!"

Jon holds his watch in front of the camera. It reads 3:05. The date in the corner of the watch face reads 6-29.

"I've given Kayla and Erin twenty minutes to get ahead of me. Now it's time to have a little fun."

Jon is walking slowly now, with the camera up to his eye, taping continuously. The only sounds the camera picks up are the sounds of Jon's voice and footsteps.

"Guess I'm not near them yet. But that's okay. I'm using the time creatively, planning a few good scares."

The trail begins to get steep, and the camera wobbles. Jon seems to be having trouble keeping his balance while videotaping.

"Sorry, folks. The camera work may be a little

jumpy, but bear with me. I believe we'll be coming upon our victims soon."

Jon hikes a ways farther and shoots a sliver of purple through the trees.

"Ah, victims in sight. That's Kayla's T-shirt!"

Then Erin's voice can be heard faintly. "We should have stuck together."

"Too late to change things now," Kayla answers. "Listen, I'm dying of thirst. Let's get to the lake."

Jon moves out from behind the tree and continues to follow them, picking up a few stones from the ground. He videotapes the girls as they slip into the shadows of the dense woods in front of them. Then he hurls a stone into the trees behind the girls and waits for a reaction.

"No reaction? Guess they didn't hear that. Let's try another."

He moves ahead, and there's the sound of another stone being thrown.

"Note that I am being careful not to throw the rock too close to them. I don't want to hurt anyone. I just can't resist scaring them. . . . If I can find them, that is. Where'd they go?"

The camera moves more quickly, but there's no attempt to focus the lens. From Jon's footsteps it sounds as though he's running. Exactly two minutes later he stops. He's breathing hard as he speaks:

"I *cannot* figure out how I lost Kayla and Erin.

They were in sight just a few minutes ago. Maybe they're playing a trick on *me*."

He begins to focus the camera on the surrounding trees.

"Hmm . . . the forest is pretty dense here, the woods darker. And the air seems, well, thick. Some kind of fog must be moving in. Not much of a picture here, folks, but stay with me."

There's a stretch where we just hear Jon thrashing through the woods. The camera records trees swathed in a dense white mist, and then we hear Jon call in a high, eerie voice, "Hello, hellooo."

Kayla then shouts back, telling him he's not funny.

"You're on to me, Kayla," he says to himself, and starts laughing. "And yeah, I probably should stop being such a jerk, but I'm going to hold out a little while longer."

The sound of Jon's footsteps and his mocking voice stops. Now we hear recorded music:

"So you think you can escape the Dark?
Don't you know, it comes for us all in the end. . . ."

Jon turns the camera in the direction of the music. The fog has gotten thicker, and the lens is only picking up the blurred shapes of trees through the white mist.

"Well, it seems we're not alone. And moving

through this fog is not easy. Feel like I'm filming inside a bag of cotton balls. I can barely see six inches ahead of me. Hey, who's there? Kayla, is that you? Where'd you get the music?"

"Don't try to run, don't try to hide,
You already invited the Dark inside.
You know, it gets us all in the end. . . ."

"C'mon, who's playing the bogus heavy metal? Kayla, don't you think this weekend is bad enough without your taste in music deteriorating?"

The camcorder keeps running, but all that can be seen is thick, gray-white mist. Jon continues to call Kayla and Erin. Neither girl answers. But other voices can be heard clearly:

"Carolyn, do you have any bug repellent in your pack? This mosquito's got my number."

"Get out of my way, man."

"I can't believe how late we stayed up last night. When are we going to get to the lake? What was Gavin saying to you before? He's so strange. . . ."

Jon pans the woods with the camera and calls out: "Hello, who are you? . . . *Where* are you?"

The voices continue talking, one on top of another.

Jon sounds resigned: "Okay, Kayla, the joke's over. You win. Tell me where you are."

The voices around him grow louder.

"Kayla? Erin?"

The camcorder picks up shadows moving in front of him. You can hear an unnerved tone in his voice, one that he tries to cover up with humor.

"All righty, I'm going to do a little scientific experiment now. I'm going to hike toward these shadows in order to uncover their source.

"This is weird as hell," he says a few moments later. "No matter how far I walk, I can't seem to get any closer to them. The fog's playing with me."

The voices abruptly stop. Jon keeps narrating, and now there's a note of fear in his voice that he can't hide.

"Okay, I don't know what's going on. Kayla is obviously enjoying this."

The distinct sound of footsteps comes toward him.

"Kayla?"

But now it isn't footsteps. It's the sound of snapping twigs echoing all around him.

"What the—?"

The sounds grow louder, pulsing. Jon pushes his way through the trees frantically.

"Okay, Kayla, I give. You did it. I'm actually scared," Jon admits. His voice moves from fear to anger. "So you can stop the spooky special effects and get your butt out here now."

Kayla doesn't respond, and Jon's breathing grows

labored. He's stumbling, caught in mist and fear. He curses under his breath, and it sounds as if he falls. The camera drops to the ground with a *thunk*. Now the picture is still and gray.

"C'mon. What is this?" Jon's voice is shaking. Other sounds come in through the mike: voices, twigs breaking, footsteps. Coming toward him.

"Where's the camera?" Jon mutters. It sounds as if he's searching through the underbrush. "What'd I do with the friggin' camera?"

There's a stretch of exactly two minutes and thirty-two seconds when all that can be heard are the footfalls closing in and Jon frantically searching for the camera.

His voice is desperate when he speaks again. "Is anybody listening?" he cries. "I can't see anything. I can't . . . Help me! Please! Somebody, *hellllp!*"

The tape cuts out.

PART VII:

The Bog

Based on interviews with Kayla Maynard
and Erin Daley as well as independent
research by Cade Merrill

18

Kayla dropped the Plague eight-track as though it were a red-hot coal.

"What's wrong?" Erin asked her.

"That boy I saw, that you and Jon didn't see, he was wearing a Plague T-shirt."

Erin rolled her eyes. "You know what? All that really matters is that we're finally at the lake. Let's get some water before we collapse."

Erin waded into the water as Kayla stood, staring at the tape. Did it belong to the boy? Had he left it here?

"Kayla! Come on! This is heaven!" Erin was scooping up handfuls of water, pouring them into her mouth and over her head.

Kayla pulled her backpack off her shoulders, zipped the eight-track into one of the outer pockets, then went to join her cousin. "Oooh! You didn't tell me the water was like ice!" she squealed.

"Who cares? It's wet! Besides, it's totally gorgeous."

"It is pretty," Kayla admitted. The late-afternoon sun was turning the lake silver and gold.

"Finding that tape makes me feel better," Erin said. "I was beginning to think we were the only ones who've ever come up here. And you know what? I don't hear those creepy footsteps anymore."

"Neither do I. Maybe we were getting delirious from thirst." But what Kayla didn't tell Erin was that she couldn't shake the sense that someone was following them. Watching them through the trees.

Erin waded out, pulled a towel from her pack, and dried off.

"Maybe we should set up the tent," she suggested.

Following Erin's instructions, Kayla helped her set up the tent. Erin crawled inside and began to lay out the sleeping bags. "I'm spent," she said with a sigh of contentment. "Time to just chill with a book."

But Kayla was too uneasy for that. She glanced at her watch again. "We've only got about an hour of light left. Why don't we just check out the bog real quick? At least see where it is. I guarantee Jon will be here when we get back." She actually believed it. She told herself that by now Jon would have realized that he was the one with the food, and knowing that, he'd find them.

"I don't know if I want to go thrashing through the woods again." Erin looked longingly at her paperback mystery.

Kayla pulled out the map. "I think we're here on the lake," she said, pointing to a cove on the map. "The bog doesn't look far at all. It's downhill on the other side of the trail. We should be back in no time."

"Kayla, why don't we just wait until tomorrow?" Erin suggested. "The bog won't go anywhere, and I'm really tired."

"Fine. You stay here and wait for Jon. I'll be back soon."

"I don't want to stay here by myself!" Erin protested.

"Then come with me," Kayla told her. "It won't take long. I'm not even taking anything with me. I just want to see how far it is." She started to walk away from the tent. Erin caught up with her, and when she did, Kayla draped her arm over her cousin's shoulder. "This is what we came to see, right?"

"No, this is what *you* came to see, remember?"

"I just want to know why I can't get this place out of my head," Kayla said. "There's a reason I'm here. I'm sure of it."

The two of them headed north from where they'd pitched their tent, looking for the bog. Finally they began to detect a faint foul odor, which gradually grew stronger. And then they spotted it.

The bog was about a hundred yards across from one end to the other. Damp, spongy earth with a strong, rank smell, like something rotting. The shadow of Metal Mountain fell over it, and a mist hung low over the ground. The air itself felt strangely heavy, oppressive.

"Let's go." Erin was impatient to get back to the campsite. "It's getting dark. We'll come back in the morning."

"Okay," Kayla agreed. This was definitely not a place where she wanted to hang out.

Kayla had turned to go when she felt an unusually cool wind kick up. The mist started to rise from the ground. In less than a minute it had turned into a thick fog.

"Kayla?" Erin's voice was uncertain.

"Where are you? I can't see you."

"I'm over to your right," Erin answered. "Come on, let's get out of here."

Kayla, hearing panic in her cousin's voice, started to move toward her. Only she couldn't. Her heavy hiking boots had sunk into the soft, muddy earth. She lifted her knees but couldn't pull her boots out of the mud.

"I can't move. My feet are stuck," she told Erin.

"What are you talking about?"

"The earth is real soft and muddy here, and I sank in a little."

"Then get out of your boots! Just untie them and—"

"I can't. I'm in up to my calves."

"Not funny, Kayla. I'm scared." Erin's voice rose with hysteria. "Pick up your feet and let's go!"

"I'm not kidding, Erin. I'm stuck. Do something, pull me out!" Kayla pleaded. She was desperate now.

"I can't see you!" Erin yelled back. "Can you see me?"

Kayla couldn't reply. She was sinking deeper by the second. The cold, clammy mud was pulling her in, holding her fast. And there was something much, much worse. She could feel another presence. There was someone besides her cousin watching this. Enjoying it.

"Kayla?" Erin shouted. "Kayla, answer me now!"

But Kayla couldn't answer. She felt something against her neck. She reached for it. And it tightened itself around her throat. Cutting off her air.

Kayla gasped for breath. She felt her eyes bulging.

It cut into her skin, winding tighter and tighter. And she knew it wouldn't stop with strangling her. It wanted more than her life.

The witch had come for her head.

19

"Erin!" Kayla gasped. The witch's grip was tightening. Kayla struggled, fighting for breath. She couldn't get any air. Around her the misty woods seemed to recede into the distance. Her vision was fading. She knew she was losing consciousness, and that once she did, she'd never come back.

"Kayla, you're having an asthma attack," Erin said clearly. "Try not to panic. Try to relax the muscles in your diaphragm and breathe. I wish you had your inhaler!"

Kayla's hands flew to her throat, and she realized that what Erin was saying was true. There was no witch. It was her asthma kicking in.

"Didn't you learn some breathing technique to control your asthma?" Erin asked.

Kayla nodded. The yoga technique was difficult and might not work, but it was the only thing she had right now. Concentrating, she forced herself to draw breath into her abdomen, then her rib cage, then her chest; hold and then slowly release it. At first it was nearly impossible. She didn't have enough air to draw. But she concentrated, fought the panic, and bit by bit felt her diaphragm relaxing. Her breathing started to normalize. Kayla felt herself trembling with relief.

Almost at the same time the fog seemed to lift a bit. Now she could clearly see her cousin. Erin was frowning and her face was white.

"Good, Kayla," Erin said. "Okay, don't move! If you struggle, you'll only get pulled in deeper. I'm going to get a branch or something to pull you out. I'll be right back."

Just stay calm, Kayla told herself. Breathe. But she was shivering now as the cold, wet mud covered more and more of her body. And she could feel herself sinking even deeper. What if Erin didn't come back? What if she couldn't find her in the fog? The air was so thick now, Kayla couldn't see six inches in front of her face.

"Erin, where are you?" Kayla called out, desperate to hear her cousin's voice. "Can you hear me? Erin?"

And then she felt a hand reach around her from behind and grab her arm. She started to scream but realized the hand was smooth, like a girl's. Like Erin's.

"Can you pull me out?" Kayla asked her cousin. She turned to see Erin's face. Only it wasn't Erin.

It was the boy!

The boy in the Plague T-shirt. The boy she'd seen in her dreams.

"Y-you're real," Kayla stammered. "You were at the car last night, and at the guardhouse today."

"Very good. You noticed."

"Wh-what's your name?" she asked.

"Dumb question," he said. "You know my name."

"No, I don't," she insisted. "And I don't know why you're here. What do you want from me?"

His eyes glittered with feverish intensity. "Did you really think I was gone? I've been waiting so long. All these years I've been waiting for you to come back, Sharon."

20

"Sharon?" Kayla echoed. There was something beyond weird in the boy's calling her by her mother's name. He tightened his grip on her arm.

"Let go of me!" Kayla shouted.

She tried to pull free, but he was strong.

"Let go! Are you crazy? I'm not Sharon!"

The boy stared at her, his gaze piercing and unreadable. She had no idea whether he wanted to help her or kill her. Either seemed possible.

She struggled against him and felt herself sinking deeper into the bog. The cold muck covered her rib cage now.

Okay, Kayla told herself. Just calm down and handle this situation. "Wh-what do you want?" she asked.

"You know what I want, Sharon."

Kayla tried to keep her voice level. "My name is Kayla. Why do you keep calling me Sharon?"

But before the strange boy could answer, she heard Erin's voice. "Kayla, who are you talking to? Is that Jon?"

"Erin, I'm over here! Hurry!"

The boy released her arm and disappeared, as if the mist had swallowed him up.

"Kayla, keep talking. I'll follow the sound of your voice," Erin called.

Kayla began to talk, but she had no idea what she was babbling as the words tumbled out. She was too frightened to care. Finally she saw her cousin coming through the mists, holding a long sapling.

"Here, grab on to the end of this and I'll pull you out," Erin said as she planted her feet firmly and held out the sapling. But Kayla's fingertips couldn't reach it.

"You have to get closer," Kayla said.

Erin glanced at the bog. "I can't. If I get any closer, I'll get stuck, too. Then we'll both die!"

"Try again," Kayla pleaded. Her teeth were chattering. She felt as if the cold wet earth were molding itself to her bones.

Erin extended her arms as far as she could, and this time Kayla managed to grab the end of the sapling.

"Just hold on," Erin said. She began to pull, and Kayla felt herself inching up out of the muck.

Kayla's fingers began to slip. "Noooooo!" she cried as the sapling jerked out of her hand. She fell back into the mud, the momentum forcing her down.

The thick muddy water was closing around her, drawing her in, holding her in its embrace.

Kayla tried to be brave, but her voice came out as a whimper. "Erin, I think it's worse."

Erin had been knocked to the ground when Kayla lost hold of the sapling. Now, as Erin got to her feet, Kayla saw that her face was filled with terror.

Kayla couldn't stop herself from struggling desperately. She knew that it pulled her deeper, but she couldn't help herself. And now only her head was above ground.

"Oh, my God, Erin," she sobbed. "I'm being buried alive!"

21

"Don't panic, don't panic, don't panic," Kayla chanted to herself. Now the mud was covering her chin. It was only a matter of moments before she went under.

And then she saw a piece of bright red cloth on the surface of the bog. It was tied to the end of the sapling.

"Grab my bandanna," Erin ordered.

Kayla fought to raise one of her arms out of the mud. She felt her body sink deeper as she managed to pull her arm free. She strained toward the bandanna and tasted muck seeping into her mouth. She started to gag, spat it out frantically—then her fingers closed on the piece of cloth.

Erin got down on her belly and pushed the branch as far as it could possibly go. Kayla wrapped the bandanna around her hand.

"No sudden movements, now," Erin warned as she began to pull the sapling toward her.

Kayla grabbed on to the bandanna. Gradually, more of her body pulled free of the mud, and she was able to reach out with both hands and wrap her fingers around the sapling. "I've got it!" she panted.

Erin anchored herself on the edge of the bog and dug her heels in. Slowly she pulled on the branch until Kayla was close enough to grab her outstretched hand.

Kayla felt Erin give a hard yank. Then, miraculously, she felt her body slide free of the bog onto solid earth. Slowly she was pulled to her feet. "Whew!" she said softly. "I'm alive. Solid ground beneath my feet. You don't know how good that feels! Thanks."

"Kayla, let's go!" Erin said. She brushed away tears. "This place is dangerous." She looked up at the rapidly darkening sky. "It's even later than I thought. The sun just . . . disappeared. Or else there's some kind of weird storm coming. We have to get out of here!"

"You don't have to tell me twice," Kayla said. She followed her cousin up another steep grade, toward the campsite. Her clothes were heavy with mud, but she didn't care. She was just grateful to be walking away from the bog, away from the boy who had found her there.

It wasn't until they were halfway up the hill that Erin slowed her pace. "Who were you talking to back there?" she asked. "I heard you talking to someone."

"It was that boy, the one I saw last night and this morning in the guard booth," Kayla tried to tell Erin. "He's the same boy I've been seeing in my dreams. I think he's the one who had the accident my mother told me about. Gavin. He must have died!"

"That doesn't make sense," Erin said. "If he died, you wouldn't be seeing him. And if he didn't die, he wouldn't be a kid anymore. He'd be your mother's age. It can't be him."

"That sounds so logical." Kayla sighed. "I wish I could believe it. But I think we're kind of beyond the realm of logic here. Erin, I saw that guy Gavin, and I felt him grab my arm. I know he's real. He's a ghost."

"Th-that can't be," Erin said. "Ghosts aren't real."

"I swear, he's haunting me."

Erin was staring at her now, as if *she* were the one who was a ghost.

"What?" Kayla asked.

"I just remembered something," Erin said. "When we did the tarot reading, and you drew that card—"

"The Death Card," Kayla said flatly.

"Maybe it meant him. Evil—death—surrounding you."

Kayla rubbed dried mud from her neck. "I've been thinking the same thing," she admitted.

They trudged on ahead, moving as quickly as they could. The sun was setting and night was taking over. They were barely able to see where they were going in the dusk. "Where's our tent?" Kayla asked. "The picnic area wasn't that far from the bog. Shouldn't we be getting close?"

Erin suddenly stopped walking and gasped. She pointed straight ahead, her eyes wide.

Lying on the ground, not ten feet away, was a mud-covered sapling with Erin's red bandanna tied to it.

"It can't be," Kayla wailed. "We've been walking for an hour now. Uphill. Away from the mists. And now we're exactly where we started. Back at the bog!"

22

"No way," Erin said. "We *can't* be back at the bog."

Kayla gingerly stepped over to the sapling and picked it up. "Well, we are," she said. "We've been walking in a circle."

"That's impossible! We took the same route we did when we came down here from the tent, except we went uphill instead of down. We have *not* been walking in a circle!" Erin shouted.

Kayla felt fear closing in on her. Erin was right. They definitely had not walked in a circle, and yet—

Just stay cool and don't stress, Kayla told herself. You can't risk another asthma attack.

"It's dark," Kayla said in a calm tone. "So maybe

we did loop around without knowing it. We just have to keep going."

Erin angrily thrust the sapling into the ground. "What if we keep walking and we keep ending up here?"

"We won't!" Kayla said more decisively than she felt. She pointed to the left. "Let's go this way."

All trace of daylight was gone now. Kayla and Erin walked in silence through the darkness.

"This place is so creepy," Erin said. "There aren't even any stars in the sky."

"Maybe it's just cloud cover," Kayla suggested.

"Do you remember seeing any clouds this afternoon?" Erin demanded.

Kayla shook her head and kept walking. She pushed the Indiglo button on her watch and saw that an hour had gone by and they still hadn't found their tent.

"Oh, no," she heard Erin moan.

Kayla turned to where Erin was looking. A sapling stuck out of the earth, and something was dangling from the end. A piece of fabric.

"Nooooo!" Erin wailed. "This can't be happening!"

Kayla reached the stick before Erin and saw that the piece of fabric wasn't Erin's bandanna after all.

It was Jon's baseball cap.

"Oh, my God, Jon! Jon!" Kayla shouted, turning in every direction. "Jon, where are you?" she cried.

No one answered.

"We're over here!" Erin called.

"Jon!" they yelled together. But still no response.

"Let's keep going." Kayla felt a surge of hope. "We'll run into him," she said. "We have to!"

Fifteen minutes later they heard the sound of the lake waves washing against the shore. And a few moments later they stumbled into a familiar clearing.

"It's our tent!" Erin cried.

Kayla stopped short as she saw the remains of a campfire burning.

Erin stared at it, too. "It must have been lit a while ago," she said. "It's just a mound of embers now."

Kayla sighed happily. "Jon found the tent and made a fire for us." She walked around the tent to the picnic table. She was certain she'd find him there, probably smoking a cigarette.

Only there was no Jon. Anywhere.

"Where is he?" Erin asked. She began to search through the tent frantically. "And why didn't he leave us the food?"

Kayla groaned, irritated. "I don't believe this! He must have waited and then gone to the bog to try and find us."

"Well, if he did, I'm not going back down there," Erin said. "I'm staying right here,"

"Yeah, we'd better stay put," Kayla agreed. "I wish he'd left his pack here, though. I'm starving."

Kayla quickly rinsed off in the lake, wanting to get the mud off. Then while Erin lingered for a swim, Kayla changed into dry jeans and a thermal shirt. She started rummaging through the side pocket of her pack, where she'd dumped the contents of her purse. Kayla soon found what she was looking for— two sticks of gum. She unwrapped one and stuck it in her mouth, saving the other one for Erin.

She glanced at the pack again, thinking about the tarot card inside. The thing gave her the willies, especially considering that a ghost was following her around.

She unzipped the pocket, reached inside, and pulled out the Death Card. Her heart raced as she held it in her hand. Why had the card been saved all these years? Why was it in her mom's old pack? Had her mother known Gavin? Was it possible that the story her mother told hadn't happened to a friend? What if it really had happened to *her*?

Erin started back from the lake, and Kayla quickly slid the tarot card into the back pocket of her jeans. She didn't want her cousin to see it. No point in freaking her out, too.

"Gum?" Kayla held out the stick.

Erin took it, laughed, and knelt down beside the glowing embers. She blew on them gently until a spark caught fire. "I'll just cook us up some delicious barbecued gum for dinner," she joked.

"How did you know to do that?" Kayla asked her. "I mean, start up the fire again."

Erin looked at her in disbelief. "You don't know anything about survival, do you?" she asked.

Kayla shrugged. "We're still alive, aren't we?"

"No thanks to you. We wouldn't even be here in the first place if—"

"If what?"

Erin hesitated. "If you didn't have those psycho dreams, and if you'd never told that ghost story to begin with."

Kayla didn't say anything. She knew Erin was right. Gavin had "called" her, and she'd come. Except he thought Kayla was her mother. Which she couldn't quite make sense of. Did it have something to do with the tarot card that he'd been holding in her dreams?

"I'm sorry," Kayla told her cousin. "I never meant to put anyone in danger, and I certainly never meant to scare us half to death. Look, I know Jon will be back tonight. In the morning, as soon as it's light, we'll all hike out of here."

"Sounds like a plan," Erin agreed, then added, "I'm sorry, too. I didn't mean to accuse you—"

"Don't worry about it," Kayla said. "Just get some sleep. Okay?"

Erin eyed the tent. "I'm too scared to sleep," she admitted.

Kayla knew exactly how her cousin felt. "Let's stay up and keep watch," she said. "At least until Jon shows up."

The two of them sat cross-legged by the fire. But after a while, Kayla realized that Erin was nodding off.

"If you want to lie down for a while, go ahead," Kayla said, even though her cousin sitting next to her was the only thing making her feel safe.

"You sure?" Erin asked.

"Yeah. I'll wake you if I need you."

"Thanks." Erin unzipped the front of the tent, crawled inside, and got into her sleeping bag. Kayla had a feeling that waking her anytime soon would be impossible.

Kayla sat and stared into the fire. Her mind kept circling back to Jon. Where was he? She was certain he hadn't driven off. Was he all right?

She heard something. Was it an animal? No. A voice? No, she told herself. It's just the sound of the water slapping against the shore.

Kayla stiffened as she heard the sound again. It wasn't the lake. It couldn't be. It was coming from the woods.

It *was* a voice. At first she couldn't make out the words.

Then she realized it was only one word.

"Kayla!"

"Jon?" she called back.

She stood up and walked over near the tent to get the flashlight. She shined it toward the trees.

"Jon, is that you?" she cried.

She heard the voice again. It was definitely coming from the woods.

It has to be Jon, Kayla realized. He's in trouble, and he needs me.

She walked slowly to the edge of the clearing. She had no choice.

PART VIII:

Gavin

Based on interviews with Kayla Maynard
conducted by Cade Merrill

23

Calling Jon's name, Kayla moved deeper into the trees. She had her flashlight on, but the beam wasn't very strong. She could only see about five feet in front of her. Still, she continued to follow the sound of Jon's voice. It was leading her along the same path that she and Erin had taken earlier, she realized. Her stomach started to churn with dread.

This is crazy, she thought. I almost died this afternoon in the bog, and now I'm heading down there again. Alone. Why am I going back?

Because Jon needed her. She was more and more convinced of it with each second. She had to find him.

The leaves and twigs beneath her feet made horrible crunching sounds. Every animal for miles around must hear me, she realized. She couldn't help thinking about the ranger's bear story.

"Please help me!" the voice called.

Was it Jon? Now she wasn't sure.

And then she saw him. He was standing on the edge of the bog, about ten yards away.

The familiar T-shirt. The shaggy blond hair. The piercing eyes. The plea for help. She'd seen him so many times in her dreams. And three times on this trip. He'd been calling her, trying desperately to get through. This time, she promised herself, she wouldn't run away until she knew what he wanted.

"Gavin," Kayla asked calmly. "That's you, isn't it?"

He looked at her strangely. "You're really amazing, Sharon," he said in a soft voice. "I mean, I know you never thought I was good enough for you. But she wanted you, and I saved you from her, and now you can't even remember me."

"What? You've got it all wrong," Kayla said. "I'm—"

"You're the same self-absorbed snob you always were," Gavin went on. "I kept telling you that the Blair Witch was real, that her evil had come to Deep Creek Lake, but you wouldn't listen. You and your friends just laughed at me."

Kayla caught her breath. Was she really talking to a ghost? Or was he real, some kind of psycho? "I'm sorry about what happened to you, Gavin. I really am. But I'm not Sharon—"

"You wouldn't believe me." He cut her off. "And you made me prove it with my life, Sharon."

"I'm not Sharon!" Kayla shouted. "I'm not who you think I am!"

"Don't you think it's time you stopped lying? I know the others believed you when you said I was killed by a bear. But you saw her. You saw the evil. *You watched me die,* and then you lied about it!"

"I didn't—" Kayla began helplessly.

"The least you could have done was tell everyone that I was right," Gavin said. "Instead you let them think I was crazy. You know what? You've kept part of me alive all these years. And the whole time I've been waiting for you to tell the truth."

"Okay, okay," Kayla said, beginning to edge backward. "I'll tell everyone. I'll contact the newspapers, I'll—"

"Too late," Gavin told her. "I don't care about that anymore. Now I want revenge. I gave my life for you, Sharon. It's payback time."

"Please listen to me." Kayla felt tears running down her cheeks. "My name is Kayla. I know I look a lot like Sharon did. But I'm her *daughter.* "

Gavin started toward her. She saw hatred burning in his eyes and understood what he wanted.

He wanted to kill her.

She turned to run, but she couldn't move. Her legs sank into thick, chilly mud, and she felt the cold muck cover her up to her thighs. The bog was pulling her down, sucking her in, holding her captive once again.

Gavin drew closer.

"You have to listen," she pleaded. "My name is Kayla!"

But it was no use.

Gavin was only inches away now. He had Erin's red bandanna stretched between his hands. And he was smiling.

24

"Let's refresh your memory," Gavin said, moving closer to Kayla. "You remember how I died, don't you?"

Kayla shook her head.

"Come on, Sharon. Think hard. It's the kind of thing most people would remember. People with feelings." Gavin snapped the red bandanna between his hands. "I'll give you a hint: What happened to my neck?"

"I don't know!" Kayla shrieked.

"Kayla! Over here!" Jon shouted.

"Jon?" Kayla couldn't believe it. She was so incredibly relieved. Jon was safe. And he'd shown up when she needed him most. She could just see the outline of his body through the mist.

"Kayla, where are you?" Jon shouted.

Gavin, too, was watching Jon. "You think *he* can save you? Ha! You should know better by now. Fair's fair, Sharon. If I can't have you, neither can he."

"Over here, Jon!" Kayla cried. "Hurry! I need help!"

"I'll be right there!" Jon shouted.

Gavin seemed to think that was hilarious. "I'll be right there," he mimicked in a high, squeaky voice. "Oh, he is so deluded. He's got no idea what he's up against."

But the mist seemed to be clearing now. Kayla saw Jon turn and catch sight of her. He wasn't far now. Can he see Gavin? she wondered.

"Kayla, thank God!" Jon was running toward her. "I'm sorry I left you this morning. I've been looking for you forever. I heard these voices—I got so freaked out."

"Jon, wait—" She stopped him. "Do you see anyone else here?" She had to know if the ghost was real.

Jon slowed, glanced around, and looked straight at the spot where Gavin stood. "Just you," he answered, frowning. "Why?"

"N-never mind," Kayla replied. "Look, I need your help. I'm . . . stuck. I can't get out of this bog."

Jon stepped closer and held out his hand. "Don't worry, Kayla. I'll pull you out."

"Say good-bye to Lover Boy," Gavin whispered in her ear. "This is your last chance."

Suddenly the ground shuddered, and a glowing mist rose from it.

"Jon!" Kayla screamed. "Run! Forget about me. Just run!"

"What?"

"Run!" she begged him. *"Please!"*

Jon turned, but it was too late.

The glowing mist seemed to form the shape of a hooded figure.

The witch! Kayla thought. Could it be?

Then she watched in horror as the mist circled into a funnel, winding itself around her boyfriend's neck.

"*Now* do you remember?" Gavin taunted her.

"No!" Kayla screamed.

The glowing mist formed a perfect garrote—then tightened around Jon's throat.

Jon's hands flew up to his neck. But he couldn't grasp the mist. He began to choke and gasp.

"Oh, no, please!" Kayla was weeping now. "Don't hurt him!"

Her pleas were useless. The garrote snapped tight.

It snapped clean through Jon's neck. Kayla screamed as Jon's head flew toward her, leaving his body writhing on the ground.

25

"Too bad, Sharon." Kayla felt Gavin's hot breath on her neck. "You just lost your knight in shining armor."

Numb with shock, Kayla forced herself to open her eyes. Jon's head, his eyes open, bobbed on the surface of the muddy bog, just inches away from her. Her stomach heaved, and she started to retch.

Gavin gave her a look of disgust. "That's not very attractive," he said. He reached out with one hand and shoved Jon's head down into the muck.

"There, he's all gone now," Gavin told her in a chipper voice. "Don't worry, he'll never bother you again, Sharon."

Kayla was weeping hysterically. "Why won't you

believe me?" she cried. "I'm not Sharon. But you called me, and I came here. And now Jon—"

"Forget about Jon!" Gavin screamed. "It's too late for Jon!"

Kayla realized he was right. She had to try to save her own life. She pressed her hand over her mouth to stop her sobbing and drew a deep breath. "I came here to help you," she told Gavin.

"Like you did that day?"

"You mean, the day you died?"

"Two points for Sharon! She's finally catching on!"

Kayla took another breath, trying to stop the shaking in her voice. "I know what Sharon did was wrong." Kayla chose her words carefully. "She shouldn't have been so mean to you. She should have believed you. But *I* believe you. I'll tell everyone you were right all along. I'll tell them that it wasn't a bear that killed you. That it was the Blair Witch. Isn't that what you want—the truth?"

Gavin looked at her as if she were the crazy one. "How can you tell anyone the truth when you won't even admit you're Sharon?"

"How could I possibly be Sharon?" Kayla shrieked. "She's my mother. *She's forty-two years old.* Why don't you understand that?"

Gavin started to laugh. "You're the one who doesn't understand. I'm not dead. Not really. I told you, but you never listened: The witch's evil works in unpredictable ways. And she wants me to have what's mine."

But Kayla was listening—to something Gavin had said earlier, to what he was trying to say now.

"I'm not dead. Not really. . . . You've kept part of me alive. . . . She wants me to have what's mine."

Something had kept a part of Gavin alive. Was it the Blair Witch herself? The need for revenge? Or was it something else? Something that once belonged to Gavin and now connected him to her mother?

The tarot card.

It had to be. Kayla's mind was racing. It was the Death Card that had kept him in some sort of limbo. And now he wanted it back.

Kayla put her hand in her back pocket and touched the top of the card. It was just a piece of laminated cardboard. Did it really have power? Could it be possible that if she destroyed the card, she'd destroy Gavin's ghost?

Wait, she thought, remembering suddenly. There was something else in her pocket. Jon's lighter! She quickly pulled it out. Twisting her body just enough so that Gavin couldn't see what she was doing, she pulled out the card and flicked the lighter. It didn't work. She flicked it again.

And again.

"What are you doing?" Gavin's voice was suspicious.

Kayla ignored him. Keeping the card hidden, she flicked the lighter one more time.

Nothing.

It was dead.

26

Kayla flicked the lighter again, cursing under her breath. Why wouldn't it work? She kept trying.

She could hear Gavin laughing behind her. "Why are you fighting so hard, Sharon? You know it's your fate to be with me. Our karma is intertwined. But don't worry. You won't be lonely. You and I are going to be together for a very long time."

Desperately Kayla tried the lighter again. She could barely believe it when she saw the spark waver for a second—then burst into a flame.

She clutched the Death Card in her trembling left hand. With the lighter in her right, she held the flame under the card just long enough for it to catch fire. But not before Gavin had closed his hands around her neck.

She felt them tighten, cutting off her air, strangling her. With one hand she tried to pull Gavin's hands from her throat. But with the other she held on to the Death Card. It was burning now, her only hope.

Kayla gasped for air. She felt her eyes bulging as Gavin choked the life out of her. She'd been wrong. It was just a piece of cardboard after all. It couldn't save her. Nothing could.

And then suddenly, Gavin's hands loosened. Air rushed back into Kayla's lungs.

The card continued to burn.

And Gavin started to scream.

"Sharon, what have you done?" he shouted.

Kayla turned to see Gavin's body erupt in flames.

She held the corner of the Death Card, allowing the fire to consume it. Just as it was now consuming Gavin.

He backed away from her, flailing at himself. His skin was blistering, bubbling. "Stop!" he screamed. "You're burning me alive!" The flesh was starting to drop from his body in chunks.

Kayla said nothing. She couldn't. This was all too horrible.

"It wasn't enough to watch me die once?" he demanded. "Help me this time! Please! Sharon, why won't you help me?"

But Kayla just waited for the card to burn completely. It wouldn't be long now.

The fire engulfed Gavin's face. She saw the white bones showing through beneath his blackened flesh. And still he screamed—a terrible, shrill, unearthly scream.

Kayla dropped the burning card as the flame reached her fingertips. She covered her nose and mouth. The stench of charred flesh filled the air, making her nauseated.

"Noooo!" Gavin moaned as the fire sucked the air out of his lungs and the flames finished consuming him.

Gavin Burns was finally dead. For good.

⋈

"KAYLA, WHERE ARE you?" Erin called.

"Over here," Kayla shouted back to her cousin.

The fog had cleared and Kayla noticed there were stars in the sky. Everything seemed . . . peaceful. Kayla tentatively tried to move her right leg. It slid out of the mud easily, as if she'd simply lifted it from a puddle of water. She raised her left leg and stepped out of the bog.

Kayla saw the light of Erin's flashlight and ran toward it. She stumbled toward her cousin and fell into her arms, sobbing.

For a long moment Erin just hugged her tightly. "What happened?" she asked finally.

"Jon's dead," Kayla told her. "H-he tried to save

me. His b-body is back by the bog. And Gavin—he's gone for good."

"Are you sure?"

Kayla nodded and shut her eyes. "It was so awful."

"I know," Erin said. "But come on. We've got to get out of here."

"I'm going straight to the police and tell them the truth," Kayla said. She sighed. "But I guess no one will believe me."

"Probably not," Erin agreed. "But I'll stick by you."

The two cousins began their hike out of Garrett State Forest.

Away from the bog.

Away from the evil of Deep Creek Lake.

Forever.

AFTERWORD

When Kayla led the police back to the bog later that day, they found no trace of Gavin Burns. They did find Jon's headless body. His head, however, was never recovered. In the Garrett County newspapers, Jon Prellar's death was reported as the probable result of a bear attack. I later contacted the M.E., who told me that Jon's head had been ripped from his body so cleanly that it was impossible to say, with absolute certainty, what actually had killed him.

One week after Kayla and Erin returned from their trip, I found Erin waiting for me outside my house.

Needless to say, after hearing her new story, I *had* to pay attention this time. It was after this that I spent hours questioning Erin and Kayla. I also managed to convince Sharon Maynard to speak to me. She was still reluctant to discuss the events of her sixteenth summer, but apparently the guilt and horror of all that had happened to her daughter at Deep Creek Lake forced her to reexamine her past. And I began to cross-check some facts on my own.

Gavin Burns's parents were no longer alive, but I contacted Bill Barnes at the Burkittsville Historical Society to ask about his nephew's death. I'd met with Bill in the past to get information about the Blair Witch, and he'd always been quite helpful. This time, though, when I asked if he thought, or had ever believed, that the Blair Witch had had anything to do with Gavin's death, he dismissed my question angrily. "Let the poor kid rest in peace," he told me. "Not everyone from Burkittsville who's died was killed by the Blair Witch. Deep Creek Lake is two hours away, for crying out loud."

I then tried to locate the other girls who had shared Sharon's cabin at the 4-H Center in 1974. Sharon hadn't been in contact with any of them after that terrible week, and the only one I was able to reach was Carrie Paige. She now lives in Maine with her husband and three kids. She laughed when I told her why I was calling. "That was such nonsense, all that Blair Witch stuff. None of us believed it except for that boy—I forget his name. Kevin something, I think. Got himself killed by a bear." Clearly, the incidents that week in 1974 were not ones that haunted Carrie.

Sharon, however, admitted that she had been disturbed by recurring dreams of Gavin Burns until quite recently—at about the same time those dreams began to visit her daughter. Kayla believes that her mother's karma somehow became hers, that it became her job to finally put Gavin's spirit to rest. The idea of helping a spirit find rest is a common thread in many ghost stories. Perhaps there's a grain of truth in it, but I can't help wondering if, in this case, it's something Kayla *has* to believe in order to make her own peace with the horror of what happened.

There's a great deal of material in both Kayla's and Erin's accounts that I've simply been unable to confirm. I sent their canteens to a lab to see if they could determine what the brownish-red liquid was. Both girls swear it had a bloodlike consistency, but the lab found no trace of blood. Perhaps Erin wasn't paying attention when she filled them up (she said it was dark in the bathroom) and the water that came out of the faucet was contaminated with rust. And, as I said earlier, I've been unable to find any evidence that explains the bugs they encountered or the appearance—and disappearance—of the eight-track tape.

Although it was clear to me that the three surviving people were telling the truth as they knew it, their stories were inconclusive. Especially when I had to allow for the fact that at various points Kayla might have been hallucinating from dehydration or oxygen deprivation due to recurring attacks of asthma.

I was about to write off the Deep Creek Lake story as "interesting but not relevant to the Blair Witch," when I came across something in another case I was researching, one that dealt with the history of Tappy East Creek, a body of water that seems strongly connected to the Blair Witch's evil. These documents detailed a 1974 highway project on Route 219, just north of the lake. The plans showed that Tappy East Creek fed directly into Deep Creek Lake before the 1974 highway project blasted through a mountain pass and dammed up the flow of water to the lake. Which means it's possible that the evil present in the Black Hills near Burkittsville flowed between Tappy East Creek and Deep Creek Lake until late in 1974.

In the end, I wish I'd paid more attention when Erin first tried to talk to me about Kayla's Blair Witch ghost story. I have no way of knowing if I could have prevented Jon Prellar's death. That's something that will haunt *me* forever, just like the disappearance of my cousin Heather.

My only hope is that each case will bring me closer to the truth.